BODYGUARD'S CELEBRITY CLAUSE

DANGEROUS DEVOTION

SOFIA AVES

First Edition

EBOOK ISBN 978-1-923471-79-5

PRINT ISBN 978-1-923471-25-2

She's one of the biggest K-pop stars on the planet. She's never been told no.

I'm about to do just that.

Cha Cha Min is used to receiving death threats. But when her newest stalker decides to destroy her dressing room, leaving a trail of destruction all the way to the stage, even she can't ignore the damage path her life has become.

That doesn't mean she's happy to see me. I'm the sort of man who gets called into situations that require a short answer and no questions about the resolution. Cha Cha hates my style, but her management team love me.

Good for them, because we won't be seeing each other for a while. Cha Cha is going on holiday.

Away from all the lights and all the fans. She'll be taking a break from the crazy while I figure out the *who* and *where* of her stalker problem.

But it looks like we brought the crazy along with us. Cha Cha is a double handful of trouble. The sort of trouble that's addictive in all the wrong sorts of ways.

The sort of trouble I love. Mixing work and play is never smart, especially out here, away from everything. What happens in the mountains stays in the mountains.

Until her stalker comes knocking and blows our slice of crazy love all to hell.

For Mum

Clothing is tossed over furniture, like she was in a hurry before she left to head on stage. A toddler given gifts, play make up, toys and gems and tantrum time. But every time she yelled at the staff, scurrying about to do her bidding was a calculated manipulation.

Just like the lyrics of her songs.

In my playground I'm the queen,
In the realm of shattered things
All the broken hearts that surround me
Yours locked away just for me,
My secret lunchbox lover.

Her voice echoes through the backstage halls as I work, the same words bouncing around in a parody of my thoughts. None of it matters, not a damn thing, as I pull apart the already dismantled dressing room she ruined before she headed on stage an hour ago.

The show has another forty-five minutes before she'll discover the fresh damage, and my message. Her entourage in the waiting room outside this one think I'm one of them, for fuck's sake. I've been invited to hot tub midnight rendezvous and orgies, banquets and afterparties. At every event, her little pack of mini sasaengs, her groupies who think they've come close enough to her but never actually...

Get there.

Not like me.

I've stepped inside her private domain. I've touched her things, and stolen her prized possessions.

Why?

Because I want to. Because I can.

Besides, right now, this is a job, like any other.

Or an obsession.

Let's see how long the game lasts before I decide not to play any longer. Perhaps I should practice and see how that final act will go.

I swing my hammer in time with the final beat of *Lunchbox Lover* and shatter the mirror that holds the message of mine that she'll never read now, letting the shards scatter across the floor of her dressing room like a fragmented disco ball.

It's prettier this way.

The hammer is a good tool. I like how it swings in my hand. The heaviness when I raise my arm. Maybe I'll use it when I crack the weighted end into her skull.

The song ends and the only sound is muted

chatter from her groupie wannabes outside who she ignores. I know, because I'm one of them.

Or, she thinks I am.

I slink outside as the power for the building fails on cue. And when it comes back, I'm just me, all over again, my tool tucked away for a rainy day.

CHAPTER ONE

DRAKE

Cha Cha Min's dressing room looks like a tornado ripped through it. Costuming scatters every surface, and makeup is scattered across her tables in a spray of colored powders. An arrangement of stuffies with her branding plastered across their rainbow paws decorates one wall. The last few dangles sadly, as though someone purposefully yanked them from their display.

Everything had been set up before she arrived for her final show in LA. From what I know about the K-pop superstar, her social anxiety drives tantrums the size of Mauna Loa, and just as volatile.

Everything in Cha Cha's dressing room tells me that today's preconcert attitude held true to form.

Except for the threat written out on the shattered spiderweb that reflects my face back to me in a million angles. Her manager stares down at me in horror through those same shattered pieces of mirror, and I return his stare.

"Bring her in here."

"Fuck no. She can't see this. It will spike her temper—'

"So you want to leave her out there with whoever did this? Because I promise you, they're still around." My thighs scream as I rise from my crouch, and take in the rest of the room with a fresh eye. "Was it this bad before?"

"Before she left..." Shayne's mouth hangs open, his expression slack.

I resist the urge to snap my fingers in his face, or slap him. "Before the concert," I bark. "Was her room this bad, or has someone ramped up the damage while she was on stage?"

Comprehension dawns, and Shayne backs up a step. Glass crunches beneath his heel. He winces. "No. No one's been in here. Right. Right?" He casts a worried glance at me then over his shoulder to where her little clan of entourage peer curiously into her the dressing room they've likely never been allowed inside before, unless sone of them are fucking her.

"Right," they all chorus like so many pastel birdies perched on a sofa, each slung around the other. A pair that were making out detach from each other's faces for long enough to shrug in tandem.

"I mean, the lights went out just before inter-mission," someone yawns in the back and I spot pink and white hair that bobbles around as the man talks. "But other than that the whole waiting thing was boring."

Someone elbows him, muttering about entitle-ment, and he shuts up.

I close my eyes, refocusing on my job and will myself not to eject Team Groupie from the building. "The lights went out? Just in this room?"

Eight sets of eyes blink at me. "It's where we've been the whole time," another white latex suited kid answers me.

"Like, sure. Where else would we be?" This one is dressed in powder blue lace.

Shit, they look like custom made dolls off the shelf, ready for a photo shoot. Maybe that's the point.

"Where else?" I echo, and glance across at Shayne. "Uh—"

He shrugs. "They'll piss in a bottle if it means holding the need for twelve hours for a glimpse of Cha Cha. The sasaeng fans club is the cream of the cream. Cha Cha took hers and turned them into her personal toy box for giggles. She even wrote a song about them. *La La for Cha Cha.* They're free marketing, and she gifts them clothes from there. These are the most obsessed people on the planet. They'll do anything to get close to her, but she never lets them."

And you wonder why she needs a bodyguard because someone is trying to infiltrate themselves into her life?

A wave of nausea slams me. "Alright. Get her in here. Now," I bark at Shayne, who jumps faster than he's moved all fucking night.

My new client needs a break. Away from spot lights and groupies and marketing. She needs time to reset her creative juices. I can't protect her from the nightmare she and her team have created in a toxic environment like this.

Cha Cha Min is going on holidays, and she doesn't get a damn choice about our destination.

∼

This is ridiculous.

I don't want to go.

Who the hell are you, anyway?

All the things I expect to fall out of the global star's mouth as I drive her away from the stadium bearing her wrecked dressing room simply...don't.

Cha Cha hasn't spoken a word to me since we left. Her focus is on the lights outside the windows of my Cadillac Blackwing. Manicured fingers drape over the leather interior like she's unsure if she should touch it or not, an alien landscape.

I don't blame the K-pop star for her silence. Shayne shoved her into a car with a man she doesn't know, and told her that her next studio dates were cancelled. Thank fuck this was the last date on her tour, or I suspected we would have had a real fight on our hands.

As it was, she came along quietly, almost dazed, as I led her through the bowels of the stadium where she performed an hour before. I took photos of the dressing room, not allowing anyone to disturb the scene, and snapped one of their management team as well, her entourage posing prettily in the background.

None of them wanted her to go, though her professional team seemed relieved that someone else took the mantle on. *Above our pay grade* didn't cover it when Shayne hugged me and pressed a sheaf of papers into my hands. A quick look told me they were threats of all sorts—obsessive promises with sexual connotations, death notices, songs fans had written that leveled from sweet to obscene. I wonder how many Cha Cha had seen, what interest she took in her personal security.

Shayne stood off to one side while he waved with two fingers and blew air kisses in her direction, his face softening. It was too late; she'd already retreated into herself, a porcelain carving on the sidewalk as I opened the car door and held out a hand.

Cha Cha looked straight at me, ignoring everyone else. Dark eyes stared straight into mine, surprise lancing across her features as she realized that I hadn't opened the back door to the car at all.

"Your ride," I murmured, flicking my fingers. I didn't offer contact, or platitudes. We'd have plenty of time to talk, if that was what she wanted.

If not, I'd do my job, and she'd continue to do…. whatever she needed to survive while we headed off the grid for a while.

"Thank you."

Her lips framed the word, and for a moment I

thought I imagined the sound that hung between us, slightly more than a breath.

Then she sank into the darkness of my car, and I closed the door.

Lights blur into streaks as the city flows past us. Cha Cha's alabaster mask hasn't flickered since we pulled away from the stadium, her focus unbroken. If she needs the time to internalize, that's great, but I'm about to fuck her night right up.

The light ahead of us is green, leading to the interstate. I apply the brakes and turn right, into an industrial area. The change in direction jolts her out of her reverie.

"Where are we going?" It's the first time she's spoken to me, beyond the looks she gave me when I held the car door for her. Hell, she didn't even acknowledge me when Shayne introduced me as her bodyguard.

"This car's too recognizable. We need something more discrete and more useful for where we're headed." I glanced sideways at her. "I wanted to give you a comfortable ride for a short while."

One glance at the silk white pantsuit she wore told me that my final destination of the trip would not be her favorite place. Shayne and her team put together a pack, and assured me she'd be comfortable with their choices. I can't imagine having someone else make those decisions on my behalf but if that's her preferred process and it gets us away from the toxic environment she exists in, then I'm happy for her.

That's utter bullshit. At least half of it. The only thing I'm happy about is leaving the building without any further threat to my newest client.

Cha Cha Min is mine for the next two weeks. That's the length of my initial contract, how long I have to protect her from whoever the hell has walked straight through her security and right into her dressing room to total her displays. Mind, it looks like she already did plenty of damage of her own. I can't wait to see her try to destroy my personal home, because that's where we're headed.

Away from the lights. Far from the glitz that she's used to.

Scant services. No internet. No tech.

I pull into the secure parking lot that reads my plates, the electronic gate closing behind us. The only spot in the five car garage is between a covered vehicle and a Jeep Rubicon with a hell of a lot of custom mods. It even has a *Built not bought* sticker plastered to the back window. That's custom, too.

Cha Cha freezes when I park in the empty spot

and open my door, hauling her small white sparkly bag from the cramped back seat of my sedan. She doesn't move as I transfer the rest of my kit to the Rubicon, then open her door.

"Your new ride, ma'am," I say evenly. "There's a toilet here if you need. I'd use it. We have a six hour drive ahead of us. The roads I take are a little bumpy."

Cha Cha stares at me, then across at my Jeep.

"Where in the hell is this holiday that I'm meant to be going on, Drake?"

The edge of fear in her voice the first time when she says my name shouldn't make me smile, but it does.

I wiggle my fingers like I'm summoning salmon in the river. Her gaze flickers, mesmerized. "Come on, princess. It's a long drive, and I'd like to get there before the sun rises. Then you can sleep."

Cha Cha's mouth moves, like she might rip me a new one. For a moment, I think she'll entertain me with my first diva level tantrum of the trip, but I'm disappointed when she slides across the seats and out the driver's door instead, ignoring my advice about using the amenities in a silent protest.

At least the rest of the trip will be interesting. I have every intention of driving hard.

CHAPTER TWO

CHACHA

The bodyguard I never hired bumps us over the rocky ground that leads us farther away from everything I know and closer to everything that apparently, he does. Not that I'm complaining right now, despite how strained our enforced silence grows with every passing mile.

Tonight's concert's strains still echo in my ears, despite the hearing protection I always use to conceal the in ear speaker that feeds my music directly to me. Unlike everyone else on the stage, I hate the constant thrum of the crowd. They might find it energizing.

To me, every fan is a vampire, sucking music directly from my soul.

Not that I've ever told anyone that. I might as well hand over my career and my remaining songs at the same time. Every K-pop star knows they have a limited life span. My band, Helium3, 'broke up' three months before our contract expired a little over a year ago. Every tear, every photograph was planned. My band mates at the time, Annie and Kie body slammed into their own solo careers alongside mine a day after the formal end of our harmonic, K-pop existence.

And then, we were on our own.

And yet, I never am.

No matter where I go, they follow me. The sasaeng. My fans. Loyal, ever present, obsessive.

It was my agent who insisted that they stay around. Take my excess clothes. Show off my charity, be a mini street team of influencers who are almost as invested in my career as me. But with a twist. I just want to exist.

They want to *be me*.

And so...we let them.

It's the worst idea in history. I've written songs about them, coded in language and twists hidden for my own personal version of therapy to clear my head because I can't say anything. Either my team is watching me, they're listening, or the media is. Or the world.

Anything I say or do is heard. Everything I say and do. Which means that I can't misstep. And in the end... I don't have to. The same agent who created the influencer sasaeng team also devised the same behaviors used to 'ruin' every dressing room in every arena I perform at. A part of the crafted Idol persona, even when I hate it.

Just another part of the act.

And now, someone who sees that same performance thinks that it's part of me and emulates the same childish behaviors until it's something far from childish at all. Something worse.

"And now I need you," I whisper into the darkness.

Drake glances across at me as the behemoth he drives lurches into a deep rut. The steering wheel jerks in his hands. He curses, a string of words growling from him that I don't follow, staring out into the night.

It must be after midnight, but I don't check my phone. He turned that off when we changed cars hours ago. Something about becoming untraceable.

Perhaps he expected me to fight. I wouldn't

know. Choices like that have been up to someone else for so long that I'm not sure what the appropriate action is right now. I stare out the window and try to imagine what the nightscape will look like during the daytime.

We left the city's glow behind miles back, and then the truck began to climb. The offer of a toilet was a good idea and I wish I'd taken it. Still, I've endured worse, packed into skintight PVC and latex costumes with hands that polish me like a second skin. The invasion of my body then is beyond forced intimacy, but I manage to endure that for a stage show and so I'll hold out now in silence.

"You didn't hire me." Drake speaks to the road in front of him.

I shake my head, knowing he's not looming, though he seems to be as aware of me in the small space of the inside of his truck as I am of him.

"I didn't know."

He breathes out hard, or maybe it's his version of a laugh. I don't know him well enough to discern the difference. "You didn't know that you had a stalker, or that you should have better security than your gang of groupies in the waiting room?"

That he gets the term right for the room beyond mine surprises me. "You did your research."

"Before agreeing to protect the most iconic voice in the world right now?" This time the sound he releases, deep and short and disparaging, is definitely a laugh. I file that away for future reference. "Yeah, princess, I did my research."

"Don't call me that." The childish objection tumbles from my lips, breathy and full of frustration. Fear, even. And now that sits between us, and I can't take it back.

Drake snorts. "If you want me to call you something else, Cha Cha, then I have ground rules. Hold on." He nods to the bar in front of my hands, attached to the dash above the glove box.

I twist to face him. "Do you think that I—"

The vehicle sways dangerously to one side, then lurches forward.

Straight up.

In ways that gravity never meant for a car to travel.

"This isn't possible—" I start.

"Princess, my driveway doesn't see a whole lotta traffic. It's been a while since I've been home, so some things have changed. Can we hold off on the tantrums until after we're at the top?" Drake yanks the steering wheel to the side, righting the vertical axis back to level, and powers us up the incline.

His drive? My mouth snaps shut on the next rejoinder. Right now, he really does seem to need to concentrate. I can wait to rip him a new one, at least for a few more minutes.

Which turns into nearly half an hour as I use the bar before me like it's the only thing holding me to the Earth's surface. I'll be dreaming of this stupid hill for the next month. My eyes squeeze shut though I have no idea how he knows where he's going, though that doesn't last too long. Impending death and I have a deal—I'll stare it right in the eye, and even though I hate heights, I glare at the darkness like it might glare back. The night is pitch outside, and the headlights barely seem to penetrate the mist that flows around the car the higher we climb.

The higher we climb.

"Are those clouds, Drake?"

My bodyguard coughs as the truck finally levels out, and the bumps stop. The engine quiets, and the only thing that's loud is my heart that seems to have taken up residence in my ears.

He grins as he reaches one hand between us and unsnaps my seatbelt. "Yeah, princess. Get used to new things. My home is your home for the next few weeks. No entourage allowed."

I'm not sure if I should scream, cry or try to run back to the city and beg Shayne to change his mind. Maybe the stalker is safer after all that. But there's one thing I've learned about my bodyguard in the hours he didn't talk to me and the rough drive up his mountain:

Drake doesn't joke. We're here to stay.

I'm not sure who I should be more scared of right now. But if I was my stalker? I'd run a long, long way.

In the opposite direction. Because this man gives off the same vibes as the one whose obsession is focused on me right now.

And he doesn't fuck around.

CHAPTER THREE

CHA CHA

Soft lighting glows along a short path from Drake's truck to the house. That still stands in darkness, until he opens it from his phone and lights that, too.

"Aren't you the snazzy one?" I murmur, placing a tentative heel on the loose stone walk.

His soft laugh at my back reminds me that I'm still not alone. Maybe I never will be.

Maybe I don't want to be alone anymore.

Out here, in the strange mountains I can't see but know are there from their all pervading darkness against the glitter studded velvet backdrop, the chill air wraps around me. The reminder of how small a creature I am has never been so fierce. Something the city, with all its brightness and chatter and white noise often knocks away.

Right now, in this moment, I enjoy feeling… small.

Quiet.

My eyes slip shut, blocking out the mountains with their heavy presence, and the cold stars above. Gravity takes hold, different from the sort that kept us anchored to the world when Drake seemed intent on killing us for the past two hours or more. This is… grounding A weight that draws me to the place where we stand. Suddenly the only presence I'm aware of is his, the warmth of the man behind me, and I know my assessment of him before was right.

He won't budge, and he won't leave. This man is formidable. Unyielding.

I pity the stalker who comes up against the brick wall of a bodyguard behind me. He won't win. But more than that—here, without all the clutter and chatter and incessant, never ending *noise* that didn't matter at all when it would stop anyway, I can listen.

And I am safe.

"Are you ready to go inside, princess?" Drake's words are soft, eking into the quiet night, but not shattering the silence.

Because he belongs here, and I'm the stranger.

"Yes. Please," I whisper, seeking permission.

From him. From the air itself.

"It's okay to be Lost," he murmurs, still unmoving behind me.

Heat warms my waist, but no hands contact my body through my silk jumpsuit. "Are we lost?" I stare at the house that glows softly, lit from within as we wait outside. There's something in that, but I don't know what it means just yet.

Drake's breath brushes the back of my neck. "Welcome to Lost Mountain, Cha Cha. I only come here when I don't want to be found."

I want to twist and look up at him, seek some reassurance in his face, but I don't. Maybe here, solace isn't something I need. I open my eyes and stare forward instead, accepting my fate, for now. "So we are lost?"

"Yep." A rough hand slides through mine. Without another word Drake strides past me, toward the house, my bag in his grip.

I trot in his wake, trying to keep up with his longer, steadier strides. Back at the arena, I didn't take the time to assess my new companion for the foreseeable future. Maybe I should have.

Drake—no last name, Bodyguard will do—

wears his suit as though it's a second skin that sits uncomfortably across his shoulders like he can't wait to shed it. Dark hair that's neither too short nor too long covers his head. His body moves smoothly in a cadence I recognize. My new bodyguard might not be a dancer, but he has the grace of a hunter. A shiver ripples over me. As though sensing the change, his hand tightens on mine a fraction, though his grip isn't painful. Just firm. It never occurs to me to pull away.

Because this man has instantly become my safe zone. It's just his driving that sucks.

Residual light from the house reaches us, the black of his suit jacket warming a little in the yellow light, mine still in shadow. I tug back, unsure why I can't keep going.

Drake freezes, and glances back at me. "Cha Cha?"

For the few times I've sassed him out about calling me *princess* already, I could do with one of those snarky endearments right now. I'm not even sure why.

"I just—" I stare up at the house, over his shoulder. It's a long way up.

He's taller than me, by a lot. That's not hard. At five feet, three inches, most people are taller than me. Even in heels. I'm pretty sure Drake doesn't wear those. He'll have to duck beneath the lintel to get inside, and it looks like it's regular height.

He faces me in full, and my heart pounds. "Tell me."

I yank my hand free. "You want me to go inside, so let's go inside."

I know I'm being contrary, but isn't that the character I'm meant to play? She slips out so easily to cover the discomfort of being the sole spotlight of someone else's attention.

Weirdly, I'm not used to someone looking directly at me. They're always too busy seeking someone else's attention, and that suits me just fine. Interviewers, media...even fans want to preen and talk about themselves. *They* are the ones before the camera. *They* are who want to be on film. I'm simply the byproduct who got them there. Even the sasaeng —at least, my version of the obsessed fans who follow me around like custom dressed mini mes— want to *be me*, not actually talk to me.

Kind of an ego drop.

Once, I wanted that. Back when Helium3 was first created, and the media smashed into me and my bandmates, being the spotlight *mattered*. Rankings, social media...it was so important. And fans.

Oh, the fans. I never understood what being a K-pop star meant until then. Sure, I worked through the system, spent years training and not sleeping and studying, all to be selected... but at the end of it all, the fans were who made it for me.

Once the media smash hit us, I breathed it in. a little too much, maybe. Then, I was exactly what Drake accused me of being. Now?

The princess act is exactly that.

"I only like being touched with permission." I stare him straight in the eye, focus wide, and stalk past him.

A skill perfected on the stage that means I don't fall on my ass when the lights go down. Good thing, too, because Drake, the master engineer that he is, does exactly that.

The garden lights turn off as the house blacks out. All at the touch of a button presumably on his phone, the same way he set everything off when we arrived.

I freeze. One misstep and I really will end up on my butt. Because this isn't a flat stage, it was a freaking garden path, uneven and wobbly. I still wear the platform wedges that I walked out of the stadium wearing after finding my dressing room more totaled than when I left it before the show.

By design. Not mine.

"Back here, princess," Drake murmurs without ever raising his voice.

"I told you—"

The warmth that encompassed my waist before returns, but this time his hands clamp down, securing me in place. My bag that he carried drops to the ground, and something inside shatters.

My naivety. Maybe.

"Here, you're safe. But that attitude? Once we walk through that door, you're a normal person, Cha Cha. It's just you and me here. No cameras. No entourage. No games. There are rules, and they're made to keep you safe. Understand?" He emphasises that last word, squeezing my waist tight.

"I don't remember having a bodyguard that was so hands on," I manage.

Lie. I slept with every damn one of them. But I'm not about to fess up to that little morsel. He'll find that out later.

His laugh is dark, and far too close to my ear. Warm breath brushes my skin in an undeniably intimate caress. "Don't bullshit me, princess. I know exactly who you are. Who you've spent the last years fucking on your team. Who you ignore, and who you toy with. Before I took this job, I did what your stalker does. Can you guess what that means?" his hands squeeze a little more, until his fingers join in the middle.

Oh, hell. I can barely manage my next inhale, and it's not my lungs that he's crushing. And it's not from the pressure. He's done his research. The proximity, the restriction, the threat…it's everything that I crave.

"You watched me. Stalked me," I breathe.

"Yeah, I stalked you, Cha Cha. You know what I saw?"

I close my eyes as a wave of dizziness hits me. My knees buckle but Drake doesn't let me fall. He holds me up, though his touch softens. "What did you see?"

His mouth touches the corner of mine. "I saw a girl alone filling the gaping holes in her life when no one else heard what she screamed above the noise of the crowd."

The warm hands let go, his touch disappearing. I wobble and I stand as cold replaces warmth. Light returns. Drake stands in front of me, my bag in his hand as he opens the door and gestures me forward as though nothing happened between us.

As though he didn't just give me the most intimate minute or less of my life, and show me that he saw something that no one else in the last years has noticed or acknowledged about my existence. Not even with the entire world watching. Not even when I screamed.

But he sees.

He knows.

"Come on, princess. I'll show you your room." Dark eyes are filled with challenge as he watches me.

Waits.

For me to crumble. Fall. Maybe he wants to be the one to catch me.

That's cute. Maybe he can. Later. Right now? I offer him a different challenge. The one I set every bodyguard I've ever had. And in a career like mine? I've had a few.

"Ooh, a tour?" I batt my eyelashes in my body-guard's direction as I sweep past him, relieved my feet work the way they should and that my emotions remain off my face. "Does it come with a goodnight kiss at the end?"

Drake's expression is priceless. Apparently my mask is better than his.

The door doesn't close behind me, and he doesn't follow me inside. I spin in a circle, taking in the heavy exposed beams in the roof, the floor to ceiling window that looks out over a view I can't see tonight. The house is open plan, huge and stunning. And it smells like...

Him.

I smile as I face him, and it's genuine. "Your home is beautiful, Drake," I say softly.

His eyes narrow, as though he's intent on deciphering my newest act.

Good luck with that, Drake Bodyguard.

Not that it matters. He won't last any longer than the last one.

They never do.

I follow him down the hall when he turns a sharp right, and leads me halfway along. The door taps open when he gives it a gentle nudge, and dims the bright light before I get there.

"Your room, princess." He steps back when I reach the doorway and presses my bag into my arms. "Uh uh. Tour is tomorrow. Tonight you sleep here." A crooked grin decorates his rough jawed face. Sharp eyes stare down at me, unflinching.

"And my request?" I can be just as demanding, but tonight, I play the sweet guest.

For now.

Drake's arched lips press together, though I'm unsure if he's holding back laughter or an insult. "A kiss from me is earned, Cha Cha. Enjoy the rest of your night alone."

He waits until I go back into the room, never breaking eye contact until the door closes softly between us.

Maybe Drake Bodyguard will be more fun than the others to play with. Maybe he'll last longer than usual. And I really do need to learn his last name.

But later. Tonight, he's right. I need to sleep before the sun starts to rise.

Tomorrow, I have a bodyguard to seduce.

CHAPTER FOUR

DRAKE

Cha Cha Min has no idea of how much danger she's in because her fucking management team never told her.

I scrunch the letters that Shayne shoved into my hand as we departed the stadium and wish I could turn them into stalker confetti. If we're less than lucky, Cha Cha's problem will develop from a stalker into something else. The letters have all the markers of a darker mind. Not just in the delivery, but the way her hate mail is structured. And from *who*. One person, specifically.

Cha Cha has many admirers, her fans who roam across the globe. Even the letters in my hand bear five different names I can research, though if I do, I'll only find three.

One is a copycat. One is obsessed.

And one is both.

Two are harmless, to my eyes. But the one that sticks out, the copycat that's not a copycat at all, presents the greatest danger to my new client.

I cast aside the letters that detail both sexual fantasies that curdle my stomach despite not having eaten for hours.

I want to fuck you until your insides are on the outsides.

I'll saw your tits off and keep them as trophies for my collection.

Your next show will be your last. I'm coming for you, bitch.

Those are standard. Two different voices written in two different hands. Neither of them worry me, especially not that last, even the more creative threats. But when it comes to Cha Cha, the concept of anyone touching her, even with their minds or twisted fantasies that will never be realized laid out on a piece of paper, leaves me close to shaking.

Perhaps getting so close was a mistake.

Tossing the rest of the letters aside, I focus on the one that bothers me most. Like the first few, it holds threats, personal details that could be generic —garnered from any press release or virtual tour of her dressing rooms or tour. But it's the tone and verbiage that slices through me.

You sang pretty tonight, Miss Cha Cha. Such a sweet voice. Soft clothes for softer skin.

Skin that will part for my knife so easily. You sing for them but I heard you. Screaming in the silence between moments of their applause.

Only I understand your voice, your greatest fan. A sasaeng of your own. I will bring you silence. Soon your screaming will stop. You'll be pretty again.

Sing for me, so I can make it stop.

Scream for me, Cha Cha.

The barb about silence and screaming settles in my chest like wire twisting about my heart. Whoever wrote this both adores and hates her at once. The letter was handwritten, then copied, as though the sender couldn't bear to part with the original.

Crazy fucker.

My job is to keep her safe, not investigate the who and where-the-fuck-for. But it looks as though this time around, that's what I'd be doing. I simply have to make sure I keep it in my pants and don't fall for my client just like her current array of stalkers, her self proclaimed *sasaeng*. Shit, I had to look up the term just to get a handle on the idea of an obsessed fan that Cha Cha and her team let so close to her. And there are more on the streets who mob every building she enters. It might be fucking anyone who sent her the letters.

I want a whiskey, but I refuse to drink on the job. Tomorrow I'll show her the letters, and tomorrow we'll talk about her security. Right now, I have two hours until the sun rises, and that's just enough to get a fraction of shut eye before I need to be awake before she starts demanding answers I'm not sure I can answer for her just yet

I place the letters on the coffee table and my phone on top, then tip my head back. From where I sit at this time of year, the rising sun will slap me in the face with the world's worst tired hangover, but the best wakeup call I can ask for without actually having to set an alarm.

For the few hours of sleep, I'll take that sun shiny, happy fucker of a glowy slap. My eyes drifted shut as I promised myself I'll analyze every letter in my sleep and what I need to do with Cha Cha tomorrow.

Trust the brain. The old adage has stayed with me

for long enough, keeping me alive so far. It will work for one more night.

Fail.

I dream of a sweet voice calling my name, and soft, warm skin I can sink into, black hair wound around my fists like a custom designed noose I make for myself.

CHAPTER FIVE

CHA CHA

"Drake. *Drake.* What the hell are these?" I snap the papers from his side table in my sleeping body-guard's face.

So what if he got two hours sleep while I turn a specific shade of branded green because I did not? I emerged from my room to find him with his eyes closed and looking serene, far more so than I suspect I ever appear. Especially right when I need company, a hug I'm never going to get from him anyway, and information on what comes next.

Because Drake's grand plan of moving me out to a mountain holiday has a huge flaw in it. Several, actually, but one is bigger than the others:

I'm a musician. I need noise.

Out here, there isn't any at all.

No music. No chatter. No instruments, no working phone, as mine died last night and no matter how much I hunt through the house, I can't find a single charger. I do, to my horror, find a wall phone that plugs into the actual *wall*.

I know he has a phone. I can even see it. He has to charge it somehow.

"Drake. Wake *up*."

Teeth baring, I shake the sheaf of letters in his face that *someone* should have shown me. "I said—"

Warm, hard fingers whip out to grip my wrist. "I heard you, princess." Dark eyes flash open to meet mine. "I wanted to see what you'd do. That temper of yours is infamous, after all."

I wrench my hand back and he *lets me*. Hmph. "That temper is..." *Not always fake.* But it is driven by anxiety, which is spiking right now. "Why did you hide these?"

Two eyebrows hike. "They were right out there in the open for you to read, princess."

My teeth snap and I wish I had a...body bit to gnaw at. Maybe for a second. Then my ire retreats and I deflate as soon as his logic sinks in. "Why did Shayne hide these from me?"

Drake stretches his arms over his head. The front of his white shirt pulls across his barrel chest, doing little to hide the planes of taut muscle beneath, or the ink that was never designed with a white shirt in mind. "Maybe he was worried about losing a digit. Have you ever shot a gun before?"

I stare at him. "No."

"Have you had breakfast?"

"No." I lower the letters I was prepared to batter him with moments before.

"Good. Let's feed you up, have some coffee, and get you learning." He rises, and I step back. The man is a giant, or I'm just short.

Maybe a bit of both.

"Coffee?" I look at him through my lashes. "Is there a chance of tea?"

Drake looks straight down at me. "Nope." His fingers twitch at his sides. "Nothing like trying something new when the sun rises, Cha Cha." The way he says my name is...final. Like he won't budge.

I raise my chin, defiant. "And if I don't like change?"

The faintest hint of a smile graces those arched lips. "Then you're shit out of luck with me, princess. This will be a hard few weeks while we work out how to keep that predator away from you in a more...permanent capacity."

My mouth dries. "There's more than one person who wrote these." The admission slips out too freely, but even when I skim over the lines that blurred together after the first glances at the letters, it's obvious that the hands are different. The threats are worded in other ways, unique to the sender.

Drake holds out his hand. "Only one of them matters. I'll introduce you to the joys of coffee, and if you're willing to listen, I'll show you how to spot a psycho in his words."

The world shrinks to the pair of us. Before I snapped the letters in his face, I lost myself in the threats on the page that I couldn't read all the way through, and then in mountains that never went behind his chair. The window is so wide, covering the entirety of the wall behind Drake, that I feel as though I might be able to walk straight off the edge of his home, and tumble into the mountain range beyond.

Into freefall.

"Take your time. I'll be in the kitchen." Drake pauses at my side. The letters slip from my hand into his. "You're not allergic to anything?"

My file will have told him what he needs to

know, but I confirm the information anyway. Some part of me registers that he asked.

"Strawberries."

I risk a glance up at him. My eye level barely reaches his chest. Drake nods, his knuckles brushing the back of my hand. Then he strides away, leaving me with the endless vista as cold company.

"Drake."

His silent footfalls stop, his presence halting not so far behind me. "I'm feeding you, princess."

I shake my head, letting my hair form a curtain between us. "No one has offered to share information with me before. They just—"

A breath passes. Another.

"They take it for granted that your world doesn't include you," he says softly.

I nod and don't reply.

Drake makes a deep sound in his chest. "Today is about firsts, Cha Cha. Some of it might be overwhelming. I'll try to go slow."

"Don't." I turn sharply on my heel.

"Yeah?" He eyes me with interest. "You want the full experience, princess?"

I hold his gaze, reading the challenge there. "I want to understand everything."

Something akin to respect flashes across his

face, and he nods slowly. "Then we start with coffee. Kitchen. Ten minutes."

He's gone, and I turn back to the mountains, drinking in their gliding presence, their magnitude. The sense of passage between. The winds that buffet even though, behind the glass, I'm protected here. If I step outside, I'll hear their sound.

Perhaps there is music here, after all.

CHAPTER SIX

CHA CHA

Drake places a coffee mug filled to the brim with dark liquid. It looks like tea, but the scent reminds me of something closer to what Kie and Annie used to drink. They both had a passion for iced Americanos while on tour, though I never formed the same addiction.

The mug warms my hands as clods sweep over the mountains to one side of the long kitchen. A long wooden bench dominates the space where Drake braces his forearms, a plate of toast before him.

The corners of my lips turn up, and he catches my smile before I can nullify my expression. One eyebrow gets a workout. I shrug. "I thought my tough guy bodyguard would have something...more. A big overwhelming plate of food." I wrinkle my nose.

He snorts and finishes up quickly, rising to place his plate in the sink. A quick wash and wipe and the plate is clean and stacked back in the cupboard. Every movement is efficient, nothing wasted, like he's...

Oh.

Drake smirks. "I'm not like your other body-guards, princess."

"How do you know that?" I snark, pushing through a wave of exhaustion that wants to drag me down like gravity.

"I did my research, remember? You've had what, five now? And you were pretty close with every one of them." His voice stays light, but the inference is there.

My tiredness is gone in an instant. "Are you judging me?"

Drake tilts his head to one side. "Judging you for screwing a guy like Major Barrett? Nah, who wants a man who texts his friends pictures of the girl he's screwing for his personal hall of fame?" he snorts when I stare. "It's a small world, Cha Cha. I was in that chat group."

"Did you share your conquests too?" I ask, in the same disinterested tone he used earlier.

Scarred fingers splay on the wooden benchtop. "If I was screwing a client, no one would know, princess. Not the media. Not my friends."

There's that final tone again, like I've insulted him by asking. Not about the conquests and brag walls, but his personal standards. Every minute I'm with Drake, I learn something about him. I study his face, how he holds himself and the connection finally pings.

"You're military, aren't you?" The penny drops far too late for me, though the clues are there. The harder brand of muscle not the gym earned stuff, the incessant neatness, both so different from my previous security. The way he doesn't joke around, how he ignores the rules, even. Because security who work for celebrities live by those rules. That's how they get jobs. But Drake doesn't seem to care about that at all.

"Ex military."

Apparently that isn't a conversation we're delving into.

I frown. "So why are you a bodyguard, then?"

He leans across the counter and pushes my untouched toast toward me. "Eat up. I want to teach you, and you want to learn. That sounds like a good deal to me, but you need fuel for that."

The toast is buttered, and it's more food on a plate than I'd normally consume in any sitting. "If I say no?" I peek at him through my lashes.

Drake pushes my plate closer with one finger, silently sassing me. "Then you're shit outta luck on both fronts, princess, and I figure this shit out alone."

I inhale slowly and pick up a piece of buttered toast. My stomach rumbles on cue, the freaking traitor, and I take a bite. The butter sinks onto my tongue and I fight back a moan.

That same deep sound Drake made before when I agreed to his terms earlier returns. "When was the last time someone made you breakfast, Cha Cha?"

I take another bite and shake my head. "I don't know." I try the coffee next, willing myself to hate it. I don't. So I try to hate Drake instead.

Fuck.

Even the mug feels heavy, and his house is too beautiful to smash anything in. Tears well in my eyes. I dip my head, hiding beneath my hair that swings forward.

Calloused fingers brush my cheek across the wooden divide. I cling to my coffee mug, unwilling to part with the gift.

"It's okay if he scares you." Drake's fingertips graze my skin.

I let myself drink in the contact for a moment before I step back. *What the hell happened to* Operation Seduce Mr Bodyguard? "I'm not scared of him."

Drake's hand drops. "You should be, Cha Cha. Eat, and I'll tell you why."

By the time I finish my toast, I'm glad that he told me to eat first. Because once Drake has outlined all the reasons why there's only three letter writers, and which ones will never actually make good on their threats, I no longer want to see food ever again.

"Is the threat sinking in yet, Cha Cha?"

I like it better when he calls me princess. There was something fun and flirtatious about his behavior, then. Now? This is serious Drake, the man ready to plan a strike with military level precision.

"I thought the sexual innuendos would be the worst ones," I whispered, blinking fast to clear my vision.

No matter what I do, I can't push away the nauseating feeling of being invaded. My dressing room, where an intruder did actually break in, even though I wasn't there; my thoughts. My body, though no one has touched me. It still feels as though a person has. Someone thinks these things about me, and I can't stop it.

I push back from the bench top, knocking my mug. Tepid coffee slops over the side before Drake catches the cup.

"Cha Cha. If you don't face him now, you won't know what sort of a man is coming for you," he says evenly as I back across the open space behind me.

I shake my head, my arms wrapped around myself. "I don't want to see it again."

"The real one?" He's in front of me in a second, and I can't work out how he moved so fast.

"Any of it."

Warm, scarred hands rest on my waist. Drake is a solid presence before me, unrelenting. Merciless. "Choose to be in denial, Cha Cha, and this threat will rob you of your peace. He will steal fragments of your sanity until you can't sleep. You won't be able to sit in a room alone and wonder if this last breath is it. If he's coming for you tonight."

My heart slams into my chest as my vision grays at the edges. I force my head back, my neck aching as I meet his eyes.

"So I'm panicking," I breathe. "Is this what you

want? Maybe this is why no one ever told me." My teeth chatter, cold sinking into my arms, but warmth radiates from my waist where Drake holds me.

"Yeah, they never told you because they didn't want you to react. Because they couldn't help you."

"And you can?" I clamp my teeth shut, refusing to let my body react. Refusing to let this unnamed person take possession of my body.

Drake smiles. "Good. That's good, Cha Cha. Keep pushing it away. The fear. Don't let it rule you."

I glare at him. "Fuck. You."

"My pleasure."

He doesn't mean it in a sexual way, though his eyes glitter, dark and dangerous. No, Drake takes pleasure in seeing me fight back, I think, rather than being the inactive diva doormat I've made a career out of, all temper tantrums and acts and stuffies in dressing rooms watched by people who don't care who I really am, just who they think they want to be instead.

"Fine, I get it. This is reality and I have to live it. So, Mister Bodyguard. Show me what you got." My chin stays up even as my bravado falters.

"Big words," Drake mutters, watching me closely. "I'm going to teach you how to defend yourself so that when that ego fails you, princess, you've got a whole toolbox to rely on."

"What about you?"

His hold on me drops away. "What about me?"

"Isn't that your job? You're supposed to be there, protect me?" My defiance switches to curiosity.

Drake laughs, soft and low. The sound reverberates around the open room, sinks into the wood that imbues with the sound. "This is me protecting you, Cha Cha. The rest of what I do? If you can see it, then I'm doing it wrong."

My nose twitches. I want to challenge him further, because sassing him is both safe and fun. He's taken what was a terrifying moment and reduced my fear to something strong and manageable.

"I don't want to be shut out of my own life anymore." I suck in a long breath. "I want to learn."

"Yeah?" He considers me. "Are you willing to take direction from me? Because what I'll teach you is dangerous, and if you don't listen well, one, or both of us, are gonna end up hurt. Can your ego handle that?" His dark eyes glitter at me like before.

He's baiting me, right after I nearly ran from him, but I understand why. Drake needs to know if

I'm going to be a catastrophe in the making of him if I say yes. But something changed last night, between the dressing room and the girl who snapped the letters in his face, the one seeking answers. Because that version of Cha Cha Min didn't understand the threat. She didn't know the secrets. And now…

"I'll listen." My words come out stronger and softer than I expect, surprising both of us.

Drake rocks back onto his heels, his face clearing. "Alright. I'll teach you what I had planned for this morning, but the lessons stop the moment you play the princess on me. Is that clear?"

He intended to show me anyway. I just stepped into his plan and threw my ego into a showdown with a man I don't understand. Part of me wants to rant and rave at that. The other half knows that if I don't play this his way, he'll clam up and I won't get another word out of him.

But my bodyguard isn't the only one who can play games. I'll listen, and I'll soak in everything he'll teach me. But he'll get the full Cha Cha experience for his efforts. No matter how dangerous this man is, he's also strangely safe. His touch is warm, and knowing. I want to push his boundaries. Maybe after the lessons are over for the day, I'll show him another side of me. The part my other bodyguards never got to experience.

I lick my lips. "It's a deal, Drake. How do you want me?"

The sharp breath he inhales tells me I've nailed what he wants from me.

Cha Cha: 1, Bodyguard…

It's your turn, Drake. Don't let me down.

The predatory look that shadows his gaze promises me he won't. I have less than a second to wonder if maybe this man might be more than I can handle, before he turns away and strides down the long hall to the opposite end of the house without another word.

And I follow.

CHAPTER SEVEN

DRAKE

Cha Cha waits for me, her perfect behind perched on a flat rock while I set up the lesson I had planned before she pounced on me this morning. The image of her actually launching into my lap stays with me as I tack paper targets to the stands that are set into the ground behind the house.

"You said you've never shot before." I keep my back to her as I work, knowing the whole idea still freaks her out.

"I've never held a gun," she confirms.

"Good to know." At least that gives me a starting point.

Cha Cha seems as determined as me to see

through this current course of action I've set us on. That keeps us both going. The bratty display at the end of her speech back in the house is something I tuck away to address later. Right now, all I want to do is make sure she learns to handle a gun safely, and aims well.

Everything else... If she has confidence after this, maybe she'll be less scared if I can't find this fucker and put him down.

Not the job I thought I'd be doing, but a call from an old friend I used to work with in the military who knows show business gave me a lead. He seems to know Cha Cha's manager too, which helps in my planning. Not that Cha Cha needs to know my intentions just yet. Right now, we're two satellites orbiting each other, but not colliding.

Not yet.

"Stand up." I stride back toward her, extracting my own hand gun. "This is loaded." I work through the parts of the weapon, letting her feel the weight, explore the safety, eject the magazine. Once she's got the feel of it and the precaution measures, we start moving on. "You're not going to fire it just yet, okay? That's your target." I stand beside her, pointing out the iron sights on the top of the gun.

"It feels like a long way away." Cha Cha's hands waver.

"It's about thirty yards, so it's within range. Line up the front post and the rear notches until the point on the target that you're aiming for is in line."

Cha Cha frowns and closes an eye. I tsk.

"What?" she asks, annoyance creeping into her voice. "I'm doing everything you ask."

"Keep both eyes open. You'll end up with a skewed line of sight, or tunnel vision if you close one, as well as fatigue."

"Oh. Sorry." She bites her lip and lowers the gun, keeping her arms straight as I showed her. "I don't know what I'm doing."

"You're doing great, princess," I say softly. "You're up to the easiest part, and the hardest. Feather the trigger. Don't pull it. It's a hair trigger, so it doesn't take a lot." I eject the magazine, and we get a few rounds of practice in with the empty weapon. "Ready to pull the trigger?"

"No?"

I grin. "You'll be great, Cha Cha. I have faith. Let's get you lined up."

Her body is tiny against my larger frame as I tap her feet out slightly and adjust her grip. Soft breaths come faster, too fast, when I thumb the safety down with her.

"Drake—"

"You've got this, princess," I murmur, tucking her body tight into mine. "We don't have to fire yet. Just breathe."

"You want me to breathe?" She laughs, a derogatory sound aimed at herself that I hate.

"Yeah, I want you to breathe. With me, princess." I inhale and press my elbows to her sides, hoping she'll get the hint and do the same.

A soft breath fills her chest, and, before I can berate her for holding on too long, she releases that and takes another.

"Good, princess. Let's go again."

Her hands begin to waver, and I cup mine under hers, to keep her steady.

Do I need to be touching her? Hell no I don't. Nor should I be. But I'm aware of her habits with her bodyguards, and I understand all too well why she has stalkers and obsessed fans. Cha Cha Min is beyond beautiful. She's stunning on another level, all perfect porcelain skin, soft and warm but to look at? She's a doll. An object to dress as others like, position how they want.

Fantasize about as they need.

I can't berate anyone for that last as I'm guilty as hell of my own runaway fantasies of the woman standing between my feet right now. When she looked at me this morning, licked her lips and mouthed off, I wanted to pull her into me, lift her onto my hips and find out just what sort of rhythm we might find together.

Keeping my hands off Cha Cha is a whole lot harder than touching her. She settles into the circle of my arms, leaning back slightly. The display of trust heightens my awareness of everything about her. Hell, if this keeps going, I'll be the one panting. I nudge her forward with my chin, and she whines softly. Prettily, and damnit, I'm hard as fuck in an instant.

"I'm not your lounge seat, princess. You have to stand alone and do this part." I step back, needing the breather before I take the gun out of her hands, bend her forward sand fuck her over the rock she was just perched on. The thought hardens my resolve to back the fuck up for the moment.

She was scared enough when she read those letters. We can play after, but right now, she needs to know how to protect herself, gain a little confidence in understanding that she has power over those fuckers who thought putting their twisted mindsets on paper and sending them to her was a good fucking idea.

Newsflash: it really fucking wasn't.

Keeping my attention on the target, I talk instead of think, because thinking involves blood flow in a downward trajectory right now. "Breathe in for me again. Now out. Got your target? Good. Then fire. Twice, if you can."

Cha Cha double taps like a pro, and my grin leaves my cheek aching. "Brutal, princess. Let's go again."

She leaves holes all over my targets, rarely missing them altogether. When she lowers the weapon, her arms tremble. "I think I'm done." She holds the gun out to me, butt first, after ejecting the magazine and clearing the barrel.

"Beautiful," I approve. "Come here." I motion her over to where I lean against the rock she sat on before. "How do you feel?"

She shrugs, letting her shoulder drop heavy. "Tired. Overwhelmed. Thirsty?"

"That sounds about right." I safety the gun and holster it. "You shot well, Cha Cha. I'm proud of you." Something that resembles uncertainty flickers in the corners of her eyes. I blink and it's not there anymore, but I swear it was a second before.

"Tell me."

Soft, pink lips part, and for a moment nothing comes out. Then—

"It's easier to take a compliment when you call me princess," she whispers. "Or when you're sarcastic. That way, nothing's serious."

My teeth clench down. "You mean it's too real like this? When I use your name, Cha Cha?"

I swear she flinches before she takes a step backward. "Maybe?"

Everything with her is a question. Okay, not everything but it damn well feels that way.

I raise a hand, palm turned upward, and curl my fingers. "Come here."

Her arms cross over her stomach protectively. "What for?"

"Princess," I offer her a single warning. "I never said we were done yet."

"Oh." She takes a hesitant step forward, then another, until she reaches where I've planted my ass on her favorite rock. "Is this lesson going to hurt?"

My teeth grind again, every inch of my senses screaming. I graze my knuckles across her arms. "When you screwed with your other bodyguards, did they hurt you?"

Her eyes fly wide, her lips parting. "How did you—"

"I know," I cut her off, not needing to go into the confessional type of discussion that will end with my explanation of how I dug into her private life before I arrived as part of her team. "So why don't you tell me about how they treated you, and what you expect from me, princess?" I use her preferred nickname as she takes a step closer, stopping between my spread feet. If I reach out now, I could close my hands on her waist, pull her into me. But it's too early and she'll run.

"There was nothing official." Black hair falls forward to cover her face, obscuring my view of her in a practiced movement. "It just happened."

"It *just happened* four times in the last two years, huh," I say dryly. "And when they left?"

She shrugs. "Then I sing."

My hands itch with the need to hold her. "You're filling your life with hook ups that you know are temporary, Cha Cha."

Her tongue peeks out as she wets her lips. "Are you telling me off?"

Am I? Probably. I rake my fingers through my hair. "It kills me that you're setting yourself up to hurt each time."

"Who says I'm the one who hurts?" The challenge in her rises fresh and fast.

I break all the promises to myself I made earlier, and snag the front of her denim top, pulling her closer. "You whisper in your lyrics but you scream in your head. I read the letters, and you know what, *princess*?" I growl, leaning forward into her space.

Cha Cha stops breathing as she stares up at me, frozen as a statue. "What?" No tremor accompanies the single word.

"I agree." I let go of her shirt, and lean back. Fuck, I need the space.

She breaths. "What?" Her breath comes faster. "You agree with *what*, Drake?"

"Come here." She's backed away from me, but I'm not having that right now. "I'm not the person you should be afraid of."

"How do I know that? You could be the person writing the letters." the words tumble out of her mouth and her eyes widen even as her hands rise to cover her mouth. "I didn't— I'm sorry. Drake—"

"Come. here," I murmur, keeping my voice low as I curl my fingers again.

"I'm sorry." She trips on her way back and I catch her wrist. It's a good cover for drawing her in closer. Not that being too close stops me because she's about to get that next lesson real fast. "Drake? Too much. Too–"

I pull her in tight, one hand closed on her wrist, the other gripping her chin, tipping her face up to mine. "You're right. I could have written those letters. Any of them."

"Drake?" The uncertainty in her eyes leaves my blood roaring. I hate seeing her so unsure in my hold, but she has to learn this. Even about me. "You're scaring me."

I know, princess.

"I could have written those letters. Hell," I bark out a sharp laugh. "I even tried, but the thought of hurting you made me sick." I run my thumb along the inside of her wrist. "I understand why they're obsessed with you, princess. I get why the sasaeng wait hours for your show to end just for a glimpse. Being next to you...it's intoxicating."

Her breath puffs against my lips almost as fast and shallow as mine. Hell, I'm driving her to another panic attack. I don't want that, but she has to know.

"Tell me it's not you, Drake." The command in her voice wars with something else. Something softer.

A plea.

We have trust. There's...something...between us and she's fucking begging me not to ruin that.

"And if it is?" I press my thumb over her pulse point. "If it is me writing those hateful things about you, aching for you, needing you but wanting to hurt you, what then, princess?" I whisper. "I brought you all the way out here, and we're alone. Because you're right. Anyone could have written those letters. It could have been me."

Cha Cha stops. The world pauses between us, around us. She leans forward, and her soft, sweet breath kisses my lips. "It's not you."

Her certainty devours me. "You don't know that."

The gentlest smile teases her lips and I ache for her, worse than ever. "I do, actually." the hint of her sweet as hell, *fuck you* attitude is back, and I'm here for it.

"Tell me."

"Aren't you demanding?" She seems to delight in the tease, holding all the power, at least as she sees it. Or maybe that's her safe zone, where I fall, for now.

"Plenty," I murmur.

Cha Cha pouts when I don't play her game. "You

called me princess," she says, as though that explains everything.

"Your safety net is my pet name for you?" I raise an eyebrow.

"Uh huh." She giggles for me and fuck if I don't pull her in a little closer.

"And if you're wrong?" Her clothes are soft beneath my hands, the material thin.

"I'm not."

"Alright, princess. Show me what you know."

Cha Cha leans into me, and rests her lips against mine. Not in full contact; this is the barest ghost of a kiss, if it even is one. I release a groan as she leans back, triumph written across her eyes.

"You told me to earn it." Her breath grazes my mouth. I ache to taste her, but now is not the right time. Heat from her blazes at me. "But also, I asked you not to call me Cha Cha then because it made me feel unsafe. Objectified. And even when you were pretending to be cruel and harsh, you did as I asked. You respected me." She raises a shoulder. "So. I get a goodnight kiss, right?" Her lips purse in a pretty pout.

I swear if she fucking giggles once more I'll burst in my jeans.

"I pretended, huh?"

"Mhmm." She sways a little, her thighs brushing mine.

I swallow hard. "Yeah, princess. You've earned that kiss. But later. It's still morning, and we have a lot of training to do. You're gonna be sore by tonight," I promise her. She's not the only one who's going to earn something.

"Pity." She turns to flounce away, but I haul her back.

"Last lesson. Breathing."

Cha Cha rolls her eyes. "We did this already."

Brat. I file that information away for later, too. Earlier, I wasn't sure about the source of her tantrums. I should be thanking her for providing me with the answer. *Earned, indeed.*

"Not like this, we didn't." I position her between my legs so we're thigh to thigh, and tip her chin up. "Don't look away. Breathe with me. Count. I'll breathe out soon, and I won't take another breath in for a while. It's controlled breathing, and a shooter will call it hollow breath. It's used for hunting and rifle shooting. Snipers use it too. But if you panic like before, and you need to take that shot, I think this might help. Okay?"

"Okay." Her teeth sink into her bottom lip, worrying it.

The note of uncertainty is back in her voice. I hate that I've put that there, but today is about a whole lot of firsts for my girl.

"Alright, let's find a breathing rhythm that works."

It takes a few tries, but we get there, matching out inhales and exhales. As a singer, Cha Cha can hold her breath for a whole lot longer than I can. I seek her pulse point on her wrist again, rubbing gently. Her breaths start to speed up again, taking my own heart rate with it.

"Easy," I murmur, making a liar of myself as my own heart rate spikes at her proximity. I battle with my own need as I attempt to calm her. "Breathe in with me. Don't look away. Out. Right here, princess. This is where we are, right now. In again. And out."

We do it again, and again. Then, when she slows with me, her pulse rate sinking, that's the last breath I take. I let the air flow from my lungs, leaving me empty and hollow. If I had to fire a weapon right now, my body holds no tension at all, and I'm far less likely to pull the shot. That was my intention with showing Cha Cha.

But instead, I find myself lost in honey dark eyes, seeking golden flecks in their depths. She stands a breath away, if that. My hand rises to cup the back of her neck, drawing her closer. Her forehead bumps mine, and our skin touches, resting together. Our body warmth melds, her eyelids growing heavy.

Drake," she whispers.

I release her and lean back, inhaling sharply through my nose. "You did good, princess," I mutter, attempting to offer her the praise she needs.

Cha Cha gazes at me like I'm her fucking idol while I'm furious with myself for not letting her get a day of training in before I fuck around with her. What the hell is the point of making a promise to myself—to *her*—if I can't keep it in my pants long enough to complete the job I was hired to do?

But let's be fair: I exceeded my contract the moment she stepped into my arms this morning. When I fed her breakfast and explained how her stalker's mind works.

When I watched her for two solid weeks without break, learning everything I could about Cha Cha Min, the moment I took the job, before I was on the payroll.

When I developed my own little celebrity crush

that's becoming so much more so damn fast. I'm snowballing into a land of heartache, while she's after a fling to ease the loneliness of her existence.

The only question is how fast I'll solve her stalker problem, and how quickly my celebrity crush will shatter this old grunt's heart.

CHAPTER EIGHT

CHACHA

I'm exhausted after my first full day with Drake. He worked me hard, taking me through self defense after shooting lessons, and driving tips after that. I sway on my feet, drinking the green smoothie he made me when I can't stomach more than part of the steak that sits on my plate, alongside a vegetable salad well after the sun has set over the mountains beyond the house.

"Fuel," he murmurs from his place at the breakfast bar next to me.

We never made it to the formal table, his house too big, it seems tonight, for two people. Instead, we eat in the kitchen, our plates lined up next to each other's.

"I can't." I try not to sound petulant and fail. "This is good." I sip my smoothie through the glass straw he's provided.

"Good? A roaring compliment from you, princess." Drake doesn't use my first name, taking the sting out of his sarcasm.

I sink into my stool, struggling to keep the room in focus. "I can keep going," I manage, stifling a yawn beyond my hand.

"Shower. Crash. Let's go again in the morning," he directs me.

I blink at the scattered seeds swimming in a sea of green goop that tastes remarkably good for the amount of kale, pear and cucumber that my body-guard stuffed into his blender. "You might be able to. I need to sleep. And...sing." I shrug. "Do something else."

Drake pauses beside me, his fork poised an inch above his nearly finished steak. Mine appears almost untouched in comparison. "I can show you the mountains tomorrow," he offers after a moment. "Take you a little deeper in. Inspiration? It's quiet," he adds. "But not silent."

I swallow a long gulp of smoothie to hide my shock. "Mind reader," I mutter.

His laugh echoes around the kitchen. "I'll plan it out."

"Your *plans* try to kill me, Drake Bodyguard." I push my plate away after nibbling at my vegetables. "I don't even know your last name. Why you became a bodyguard. Or who you were in the military."

Drake spears his last piece of steak, emptying his plate and chews slowly. He finishes his meal, and collects my plate without a word, taking them away. After he's cleaned up, and I've slipped on my stool, ready to fall asleep at the bench, he catches me, turns me in his arms, and leads me along the hall toward the bedroom I used the night before.

"What happened to the shower suggestion?" I swipe a hand across my eyes, but the hallway stays blurry. "Why am I so tired?"

"Because you barely slept, then I worked you like a special ops trainee, princess. You held up pretty well. Got a little dirty, didn't complain half as much as expected." Approval coats his voice.

I hate that I crave what he offers me.

"I'm storing it up for tomorrow," I sass him. "Watch out for that hike, Mister Tough Guy."

"Yeah? Think you'll take me?" He sounds amused as he opens my door.

"I might surprise you." I'm lying to no one. The only thing I'll take right now is the first pillow in sight and a blacked out room.

"I'd like to see that." The humor dissipates from Drake's voice as he leads me into my room by my hand and turns my covers back. "You pack pajamas, princess?"

I snort. "I didn't get a choice on what went in my suitcase, and unless you consider latex or leather pants sleepwear, then the answer is no."

His lips twitch. "Maybe another time, then," he says softly. "Hop in."

"I'm filthy." The innuendo in my words hits me way too late.

Drake ignores the option to snark at me for one. "Probably, princess. But this bed has seen far worse. Crawl in. I'll fix your sheets tomorrow."

"Story?" *Kiss?* I want to batt my eyelashes, but my body refuses to work the way I want it to behave. I crawl in as Drake suggests, and he tucks me in.

The light flicks off, and he leans over me. "I thought you wanted something else."

He doesn't pose it as a question, so I don't answer it.

"Tell me what you did in the military."

Drake's hands still on the blanket over my shoulders. "I was a medic."

I focus on his silhouette, unable to see his face. "Were you good?"

"Always."

The lack of ego in his easy response tells me he probably was good.

"Why did you leave?" I find his hand over the blanket with mine underneath and work my fingers under his.

He lets me and gives mine a squeeze. "Story time, huh?" he mutters. "The kiss would have been easier." A heavy breath leaves his chest. "We were in —" Drake coughs. "A shithole. I patched our team up more times than I should have, but they were still breathing. We were four hours from extraction. From sending us all home. Safe ground. Then two. One." His hand tightens on mine.

"Drake," I whisper, wishing I hadn't asked.

His head tips down, his face obscured by shadows. I'm not sure if he's looking at me or seeing the scene play out before him. "We had a young soldier. Redman. I don't remember his first name. He took a shot to the thigh. I patched him up, too. The plane arrived. Never powered down. We ran, fucking pink dust everywhere, kicked up by bullets pinging the ground and the turbines. I can taste the dirt mixed with metal and blood when I close my eyes." His hand closes on mine.

I don't break into his story, don't interrupt. I asked for this, and he's telling me. Listening is the least I can do. I wonder how many times he's told the story about the soldier Redman, or ever.

"Everyone got on the plane. It was a fucking miracle. We couldn't believe it. Statistically, someone should have been shot, but...no one was. So we cheered as the plane took off. It was a small incursion. They had no ground to air missiles and we launched safely. Got into the air. I talked to Redman the entire time. Took me three fucking minutes to realize he wasn't talking back."

"He was gone." I squeeze his hand through the blankets, unable to free myself from the knots.

Drake jerks, finding reality, maybe. "Yeah. He fucking bled out sometime after we got on board, or maybe as we were running. I don't know. I've played it over and over in my head a million times. I carried him, because it was my job. I lifted him in and fucking cheered while he died and *I didn't know, princess.*

"I watched a lot of men I loved die in circumstances that they couldn't control, princess." He squeezes my hand again, his voice smoothing out. A kick in it, like he's granting me permission to sass him. Begging, almost. Anything to ease the tension.

I wish I didn't ask for a story, but I'm glad that I know his. And now it's my turn to bring him back. I search for words to lighten his mood, but everything seems pithy after that.

"And now you choose to offer security to divas who throw stuffie tantrums in dressing rooms. That's a new sort of war zone," I offer, cringing internally at my choice of distraction.

Drake barks a harsh laugh. "I'll take the stuffie war and raise you a stalker, K-pop queen," he murmurs, dispelling the mood in a second.

His talent, taking panic, fear and dissipating it. I can imagine what he would be like amidst the chaos and madness of what he's described.

The hand gripping mine releases, flexing. "Working in independent security means I get to pick what jobs I want to do, who I'm working with. People I can trust. Clients I like."

"How do you know you like me? We just met." It seems a reasonable thing to ask, but I'm already fading. Maybe I should have asked for a kiss, not a story. Tonight, I think he might have capitulated after all.

"I watched you," he says simply. "The moment that I knew you were mine, I learned everything I could about you. Who you were, what you wanted the world to see. What you didn't. I learned everything, Cha Cha." My breath stalls when he uses my name. "And the woman I saw on that stage, when I listened to every song you've ever written? I think —" Drake cuts himself off, reaching up to swipe hair back from my face.

I lie frozen beneath my blankets, trapped there under their combined weight and his leaning over me. "I haven't released all my songs," I whisper. "You don't know everything. I promise."

Light from his phone illuminates his face. "I do, princess. I found those songs, too." the fingers seep through my hair. I read every one of them. Listened to the recordings that you haven't released yet. Everything about you is beautiful."

My breath shatters in my throat. I'm not sure if I want to scream or cry. "Those songs and recordings are at my house. My home."

Drake's hand cups my cheek. "They are."

Breath leaves me empty. Airless. "I wasn't there—"

"You were on tour. The first weeks." He says it so evenly. So normal.

"Drake." My heart pounds as I try to free my hands from the blanket, and only succeed in tangling myself into a knot. I struggle as he strokes my hair back from my face so gently.

"Breath, princess," he murmurs. "With me."

"But you– you—" I can't get the words out.

"In with me. Out," he encourages, until my chest loosens and the panic attack passes. "That's it. Now, say it."

He knows. He *knows* what I'm going to ask and he's asking me to say it.

I can't.

I have to.

Darkness shrouds Drake's face. His touch is so light as he trails his fingertips through my hair. I want to lean into his palm, the hands that, until moments before, I thought were safe.

"Why?"

Why did you break into my house? Why did you invade my life?

"That's not the question that you want to ask, Cha Cha," he berates me softly. Even though he uses a gentle tone, there's no denoting that I'm in trouble.

I choke up again. "I—"

"You can ask me," Drake murmurs. "It's okay, princess."

"Didyouwritetheletters?" I blurt it all out at once, my question unintelligible and rushed.

But it's out there.

Drake's touch stops. His hand retracts.

I wait.

"No," he says softly.

I close my eyes. A sob escapes. "Why were you in my house?"

"Because I wanted to see how easy it was to break in. It was easy as hell, princess. We have a lot to talk about your security measures. Whatever the other bodyguards put in place, it's not worth shit. And because it was far too easy to become obsessed with you." he leans down and presses his lips to my temple. "I'm in the room across the hall. If you need me tonight, if you're too scared to close your eyes, I'll sit in the doorway. No closer. I promise," he whispers against my temple.

Breath shudders from me. "I was safe with you," I whimper.

"Was, princess?" He cups the back of my head tilting me back, exposing me. "We're gonna go over every entrance point in your home tomorrow.

Together. Then the dressing room situation, then the sasaeng, maybe your staff on your management team as well."

"I thought we were hiking?" I shiver as he leans over me, caging me in though there are blankets between us and our bodies never touch.

"We can do that too. First?" He massages my nape as I nod. "I promise, princess. We can get through this."

Some part of me believes him, because I want to. Some part of me is as addicted to this man who slid into my life by both effort and design.

And some part of me wants to trust him because I can, despite how dangerous I know he is. Because even though he's known me for far longer than I have known him, I can't help but crave Drake.

And that's a dangerous feeling that sinks deeper under my skin.

"Sleep with me?" I whisper, knowing it's not what he offered at all, but it is what I need tonight.

I sense his smile, his victory before he speaks.

"Not tonight, princess. But I'm real close. I promise. For now, close your eyes."

He settles on the floor beside the bed, the carpet muffling his movements. My eyes shutter, but the scent of him, something earthy and metallic, is a constant reminder that he's there. I fight with the blankets again, pushing my hands free of the knot until I achieve success. Shoving them aside, I reach out blindly and clip his shoulder.

"Sorry," I whisper, reaching for him again. "I didn't mean to hurt you."

"You didn't." His tone is reassuring, his grip as he laces our fingers together firm and warm. "Sleep, Cha Cha. I won't go anywhere."

I stare at the ceiling I can't define in the darkness for a moment longer before my eyelids are too heavy and droop.

Then only darkness and warmth are my company, warding away night wraiths dressed in hoods and masks with faces so horrific that I wake up with my scream still stuck in my throat more than once.

And every time, I find Drake still leaning against my bed, his hand wrapped firmly in mine.

I never pull away, and neither does he.

CHAPTER NINE

DRAKE

The soldier's name was Jimmy Redman.

I lied to Cha Cha. I do remember him, every aspect, from the kid's puppy brown fucking eyes to the name his mumma gave him. My legs pound the rocky ground surrounding the house just after daybreak as I sprint the track my body knows well. Anything to remove the memory I thought I buried but managed to exhume last night because she asked.

Not that it's her fault. I decided that was the nighty night tale I'd tell her. Shit, I should have kissed her instead. Then I fessed up to being her stalker—one of—even if it was for a good reason.

Ha. Breaking Cha Cha's trust hurt more than I thought possible. Two fucking days with her, and I'm already well embedded into her sasaeng fan club.

Sign me up for the next tour.

Maybe her management team can put me in the waiting room with her pastel colored crew and lend me a costume to blend in.

I stop just above the house, staring down at the building. I bought the property when I left the military, needing somewhere to remove myself from the world. Hide from memories that haunted me, when being around people wasn't the right place. Then, I slammed my feet into the track that I run now, with the house in plain view. There's a much longer one that I'll take her on later, that winds deeper into the mountains. The stunning views and quiet winds that speak of silent strength and sleeping gods beneath the soil will hopefully be enough to combat the nightmares Cha Cha suffers from.

They once were for me, and I hope this place will be the same for her.

I was selfish in bringing her out here. Hell, with her security budget I could have taken her anywhere in the world, hidden her on any continent. But Cha Cha is hellishly recognizable, and this is ground I'm intimately familiar with. Here, I'm king. Here, I know the land, and can protect her.

Here, she's queen.

Shadows flicker across the windows inside the house. The movement means she's up. Huh. I knew Cha Cha rose early on tour days, but I figured she kept those hours out of anxiety. Apparently, it's a regular habit, or maybe I was right the first time and it's a cycle she can't break.

I jog down to the house, breaking off the track and enter through the back door, locking up after myself. Here, there's no threat to her, but the need to keep her safe against the man I know will come for her is too strong. Even here, I'm all too aware of her needs to become blase.

Soft notes reach me as I unzip my jacket and hang the garment on a nail inside the door. Cha Cha toys with a melody I don't recognize. I didn't lie to her last night when I told her I'd listened to her entire unpublished catalogue. She circles the living area, her head down, her face obscured by her hair as she writes notes on a notebook. Hell, she's wearing my shirt, a grey one from my military days. The material hangs loose over her frame almost to her knees, like a dress.

When I glance at her legs, I get why. She was

right; whoever packed for her while she was on stage picked...for a tour. Her legs are encased in black leather pants.. My mouth dries and I force my gaze higher. The full picture of her, leather pants, wearing my shirt, long black hair draped along her back...hell, she's a sight. My cock kicks in my pants, the exhaustion of my run forgotten as my blood heats.

Cha Cha writes on, scribbling notes and singing softly to herself, oblivious of my study. I smile. Her home was full of handwritten notations, pages and Post Its everywhere. Most were in shapes of stylized flowers and animals, covered in lyrics she'd written in circles or ribbon shapes as though the music flowed from her in waves.

Grabbing a full water bottle and topping it up with a dose of electrolytes, I slug it back as I lean against the wall, watching her. Fuck, having her in my home is intoxicating. More than that. Seeing her create as she walks about, scribbling frantically, trying different wording...Christ, she's beyond beautiful.

Nothing in my research trip promised me that the woman the world obsessed over—myself included, with my little crush developing daily in the two weeks I spent understanding who she was and the holes in her life—would slide into my world that differs so drastically from hers.

Cha Cha comes from a glitzy landscape where I'm far more rough and rustic. My history is brutal and hers is all auditions and tours. The one thing I've learned about her is that we both understand that work isn't something we can shut off. It's what we do, what we live. That's the single commonality between us.

Her head raises, drawn out of her reverie. "You are a stalker," she reproves me, though there's nothing fearful in her voice.

Tension flexes across my shoulders at being caught out. The slightest smile curves her lips, and I relax, leaning back.

"You like stealing my clothes, princess?"

The hint of a smile becomes a full blown bratting out smirk as she peers up at me through her lashes.

Fuck me, that look should be illegal.

"You don't want to see the top that pairs with these pants." She kicks out a leg to demonstrate the leather that encases her like a second skin.

"Mmm." Given permission to look, I do, sliding my gaze over her body.

Cha Cha tips her head to one side, unresistant as

she returns the favor. It's been a while since I've been aware of a woman checking me out. Usually, I do my job, and move right along. My scars—the ones both ironside and out—are baggage enough to weigh me down. Low enough I wonder if I'll ever emerge. But Cha Cha digs her way under my skin, giving me reason to care. I close my eyes and inhale.

The difference of having her in my home is there, but it's subtle. Something softer, sweeter. Like my house has been too harsh without her here. Missing her.

"I like the new song." I keep my eyes closed, and don't need to open them to know she's creeping closer. Her soft footfalls are quiet, but she's not silent.

"It's not finished yet."

"So finish it."

"I thought we were going hiking."

The warmth of her slams me, even though we're not touching. My palms ache to reach out and pull her into me, but I know that will frighten her. "You need to complete it, right?" I let my eyes drift open lazily, staring down at her. She nods, looking up at me uncertainly. "Then we stay. I can fill the time."

She worries her lower lip. "I can just...write? I won't bother you?"

Damn, she's prettier up close than on stage than in her pictures.

"No, princess. My home is yours. Use it how you need. If you want a break, I'll be around."

Her lips flicker. Once. "Stalking me."

If that's what you need to call it.

"That's right." I fold my arms and don't move.

She leans forward. "You need a shower, Drake Bodyguard."

I huff a laugh. "Is that a prerequisite for your songwriting abilities?"

"Yep." She swings away, sashaying her hips in those torturous leather pants.

I swear my old shirt never looked so good.

Cha Cha's music fills my home day after day. I feed her, and she sings. I swear the wind that slides between the mountains visits just to answer her.

Out here, where there's no neighbors for miles, the only sounds are the creaks from the trees near the house, the occasional wild animal who don't come near us, and her.

Having company is a different experience for me, too. I know from Cha Cha's history that she's rarely home. It's why I chose to invade her home when I did, when she was on tour. The right thing to do? Hell, no. An example of where her security needs a level up, or five?

Abso-fucking-lutely.

I run through the plans of her house that I printed out earlier in the week as she watches me, picking at her ramen. I'm yet to see her eat a full meal, but I'm working on it. The more energy she has, the harder we can train together. I refuse to let Cha Cha leave without knowing she can defend herself if I'm not around. That thought gives me pause, and I raise my head to find her watching me.

"You're supposed to be eating, princess," I say softly, breaking the pervasive silence that falls between us.

Night obscures the mountains outside, the glass reflective. We never did get that hike in together. I pencil it in mentally for tomorrow. Getting outside is good for her, and she should know the terrain if we stay here much longer.

Cha Cha leans forward and slurps her noodles. Damn, that's another action I can watch all day. Just being near her is addictive. She finishes up, and pushes her bowl aside. I expect sass, but that's not what tumbles from her puffy lips.

"Have you received any more letters?"

I cock my head to one side. "What makes you think I'm checking?"

She handed her email accounts over to me a few days ago, unwilling to see the evidence land there herself. Not that either of us expect the stalker to hack her; it's Shayne we both expect to hear from. There's been radio silence from her management team since the night I took her away from the stadium where the man who hunts her broke into her dressing room and destroyed her things. Shattered her mirror.

Wrote the message on the glass before he splintered it apart.

Cha Cha fixes me with a challenge she knows I won't back down from. "You're checking."

I laugh. "Yeah. I am." I pick up her bowl and wash it, avoiding her hands when she tries to help. "No, there's nothing. Not a thing, Cha Cha. I'll tell you if there is." I put the bowl away and turn back to find her still studying me.

"Will you?"

I let the quiet between us settle until it becomes too much. Bracing my elbows on the wooden bench top, I lean toward her. Tonight, she's paired yellow latex pants—another prime pick from the team management pack—with a black knit halter top. There's nothing beneath it, her body soft and free as she moves, swaying unconsciously toward me.

We've spent the last week orbiting around each other while she finishes her songs, producing one after the other. It appears that with the reduction of glitz, glam and distraction, Cha Cha is a power-house, discovering inspiration in everything.

I smirk, trailing my gaze over her pink stained cheeks to her lips that she licks. "I'm taking you on that hike tomorrow."

"Hike?" Her gaze, unfocused, snaps back to meet mine. "What hi—oh."

"Yeah. Oh." I straightened. "Your songs are done, right?"

She nods. "I finished the last one this afternoon. It's not perfect, and I need to tweak it with equip-ment, but... the bones are there."

"Good. I'm glad you aren't sitting around, stressing yourself stupid out here, Cha Cha." I soften my voice to take the edge off my words.

"Me too," she whispers. Cha Cha slides off her stool, heading away from the kitchen. A few steps from the hallway entrance, she turns back to me. "Tuck me in after I clean up?"

My mouth dries, and I nod. "I'll be around." I let her get a few steps further away. "Princess."

She half turns back, already lost in the shadow. "Drake?"

"I'll tell you if anything comes through."

She sways into the light, enough for me to see the smile that changes her face. "I trust you."

Then she's gone, and I'm left with a raging hard on and a fantasy I'll play out with her against the wall of the spare bedroom she's slept in for the past week. Hell, I thought we'd never hit this point. The flirting ceased once she started songwriting, and I let her be, knowing it's what she needed.

Being around her is enough, but aching there constantly, unable to touch...that's a different form of torture. She stopped asking for goodnight kisses then. I slept across the hall from her after the second night I spent on the spare bedroom floor, my hand tangled in hers. Knowing she still wants me is more than I can ask.

Now I just have to accept that when we're done, she'll move onto the next bodyguard while I'll still crave her. Hell, I'm as bad as any of her tame sasaeng, for fuck's sake. Here she is in my house... fucking her is the worst idea possible. But I won't say no, and I'll make sure she remembers tonight.

Forever.

CHAPTER TEN

CHACHA

Drake is intimidating beyond belief. I've spent the last week talking myself into avoiding the man who watches me even when I think I've managed to find a place where he can't see me. But then that's his job, and every time I turn around, there he is. It's become a game between us: where can I hide in his house that he can't find me?

Answer: nowhere.

By the end of the week, I'm okay with that. Drake is far more attentive than any of my previous bodyguards, actually earning the title. When I write, he's there, somewhere in a corner of the room. Not impinging on my space, just present. And after a while, I'm used to him. He stopped training me once I started to sing and I get the impression that he...

Listens.

A huge part of me likes that. Loves it, even. That might be an ego trip, but I don't think so. The sense that he's there leaves me desperate to turn to him for more. The first night he didn't stay in my room, I lay awake, trying to make out the shape of the mountains in the darkness beyond. But the moon was dark that night, and all I could see was the outline of the trees just outside my window. The concept of crawling into his bed was terrifying.

Now? I bite my lip as I wash my face and brush my hair back, letting it tumble freely over my shoulders. Now, I want to strip bare and slide beneath the covers of his bed, just to see what he'll do.

Probably turf me right back into my own, and go back to watching me, sans pet name. He's still intimidating as hell. I'm simply ready to risk that wrath now.

Or desperate enough.

"Ready for bed, princess?" Drake rests one arm against the doorframe above his head. His black t-shirt rides up, exposing hard, defined musculature.

The innuendo in his words is not lost on me.

I place my brush carefully on the stone benchtop, tugging at the hem of my top. I'd meant to change out of the latex pants before he found me, but I'd been lost daydreaming about him and run out of time.

That's one of the things I love about Drake. He refuses to work to anyone else's schedule, including mine. That he gave me time to play around with my songs was a gift, one I never get with my home or rented apartments stuffed with people who shouldn't be there but are anyway.

One I won't squander.

I raise my chin. "I'm ready."

"Good," he says softly, holding out a hand.

I stare, my heart beating too fast. The last time he offered me his hand was the second day here, and when I took it, he reeled me into him. My heart beats too fast in my chest, leaving me breathless. *Breathe.* Another lesson from that day.

Shutting my eyes, I take his hand and wait.

Drake huffs out a sound that might be a laugh, or something else. "Come on, princess. I made you a promise." He tugs gently, his grip firm on my fingers.

It takes a moment, then I realize he's leading me along the hallway. "I thought—" I follow him, trying my best not to trip over my own feet.

Drake stops at my doorway, his bulk filling it as he gazes down at me. "I know what you thought."

"Oh." I don't know what else to say under his unyielding stare. I edge around him, through the tiny space he leaves for me to get through, and into the room, only to find I can't go any further because our hands are still entangled. The pressure of his fingers on mine feels so good that I don't want to pull away, but if this is where I leave him, then letting go is the only option.

"I don't want to," I whisper into the empty room without meaning to voice the words.

"Then don't."

Drake's other hand glides along my arm until he grips my shoulders. He doesn't turn me as he steps into the room, kicking the door shut behind him. I jump as it slams in its frame. The walls swirl around me before my back is pressed to the door's hard, cold surface. A cry tears from my throat. I clamp a hand over my mouth, unwilling to ruin my voice.

"You—" I'm not sure what I'm fighting as I push forward, but my hands hit nothing at all, slapping at the air. "What are you doing?" I pant, scrabbling at Drake's dark hair as he kneels before me.

He gazes up at me with the sort of adoration and worship I've seen in the eyes of the audience, from fans when I'm on stage a hundred times, though never this close. "Giving you the goodnight kiss you've been begging me for, princess."

I want to argue that I haven't been *begging* him for anything, or that he's in the wrong position. But when his mouth presses to my pussy, bare beneath the restrictive latex pants, the sensation is so much more than I've ever imagined. Drake closes his mouth gently over my mound, his tongue and lips working sweetly to French my pussy in simulation of what he might do to my mouth.

The latex acts like a second skin, enhancing every touch, and Drake knows exactly what he's doing. A scream builds behind my lips. I clamp my hand over them but it's too late. The moment he swipes his tongue across my clit, my preoiled skin, needed to slide into the latex in the first place, is already wet and ready to go. I come under his knowing kisses, my knees buckling as he flicks at my clit over and over.

Heat explodes between my thighs as I pant for him, but he doesn't stop, sucking and licking and kissing. His tongue probes my entrance, and I moan at the depravity of him unable to push inside me.

"Drake," I whisper, opening my legs. "I want you inside me."

He doesn't answer, doesn't take his mouth from me, only picks up one leg, tossing my knee over his shoulder. His mouth pins me to the door, the pressure of his kisses and sucks driving me to the edge of bliss again already.

I whimper, riding his mouth as he finds the perfect place to flick. My clit hardens under his ministrations. Twisting to get away from him doesn't work, the sensations too much. He clamps his hands on my hips, holding me open, in place, and goes back to work. I scream my way through a second orgasm, losing all sense of who I am and where.

My body convulses. His warmth surrounds me everywhere.

"I got you, princess," Drake murmurs, hauling me into his chest. His heart beats close to mine, his hands knotted in my hair.

I don't even care that it's a mess for once. "Can you do that every night?"

"Every night that you need, Cha Cha," he murmurs, tipping my head back. "Wear those pants and I'll lick and kiss every inch of you."

I swallow at the image of him, slick coating the insides of my thighs. "And fucking me?"

"Christ," he growls, sliding one hand free of my

hair to coast along my side and grip my hip. He pulls me sharply into him, seeming to relish the cry he draws at the action. "Two orgasms isn't enough for you tonight?"

I squeeze my thighs together, but the latex doesn't do half enough to ease the ache inside me. "I want you," I whisper.

He traces fingers across the front of my pants, sliding over the damp spot where he licked and kissed me and forced orgasms from my body. A few strokes and he presses in quickly. I arch up, but my hips press forward, wanting *more.*

"How wet are you, princess? You feel so goddam hot," Drake mutters. "If I peel these off you, you're gonna soak me."

Heat stains my cheeks. "I had to oil myself to get them on," I whisper, unsure if that's the answer he wants. "It's a trick we use on stage. It's easier to slide…"

"Everything on," he growls, rubbing me gently. I work my pussy against his hand, mewling softly. "Fuck, you gonna cum for me again, Cha Cha?"

"Yes. Please. Don't stop," I beg. A deep noise rumbles in his chest when I nod, panting.

"So cum for me. But if you don't, I'm gonna leave you in these pants, wet and soaked, all fucking night. Aching and wanting, and empty. You get yourself off for me, and maybe I'll play nice and fuck you like you want. Can you do that?"

I pant harder, the room growing hotter. I swear it shrinks, darkening at the edges. Drake's touch is lighter. I chase his fingertips with my hips, rolling them as I seek the pressure I need.

"Please," I mewl, unable to make sense of anything.

"Yeah? Tell me what you need, princess." Drake never stops, but he doesn't give me what I want, either.

I gasp out my frustration when he laughs, and straddle him. His eyes widen, and his gaze travels over my body. "I need to ride you," I manage, rubbing my body against his harder one, taking what I need when he refuses to give it to me.

"Christ, Cha Cha. If you don't stop, I'm gonna —" He cuts himself off with a curse. One fist, knuckles up, presses against me, over his lap. "Grind that pretty little pussy on me. Show me how you make yourself come and I'll give you every fucking thing you need."

I spread myself wide over him, finding the angle I need and press down. His knuckles drive into my clit, the hard, scarred ridges providing the perfect pressure. My hands close on Drake's shoulders for purchase, fisting his shirt. "I want you inside me so deep I'll never want anyone else." The words tumble free, but I know they're true the moment I say them.

I've never trusted anyone like I do Drake, no matter what he's done. He watches me like I'm something precious, not like I'm a trophy for his wall or a bragging point for his gym buddies. He watches me like I matter, and he listens to me like I'm human.

And his touch…

His touch is designed for one person.

"That's what you want, princess? Just me?" His eyes are laser focused when I meet his gaze. His other hand knots in my hair, close to my scalp, locking me in place. "Promise that's what you fucking want."

I cry out, the edges of bliss obliterating reason. "It's you I want," I whimper. "Just you, Drake. Watching me, seeing me. Being here with–" Breath stalls in my lungs.

He jams his fist deeper into my crotch, hard enough to bruise tender, swollen flesh from the orgasms he gave me earlier. The latex protects me, enhancing the sensations. My clit throbs, like it might burst.

The sound that tears from me might ruin my voice but I can't help it. "Drake," I scream, the wave edging into me, so sensitive, so close and I can't stop. Our bodies rock together, tight and hard.

He curses, grinding into me with his fist. "Fucking cum for me, princess. I'm yours, always."

I close my eyes and let go. Let him hold me as I fall. Heat drenches me inside and out. A scream fills the room. I know it's mine, though I don't feel it. Only the pleasure that courses through me, the feeling trapped by the restrictive latex pressing the tortured nub of nerves tight back to my body.

Drake growls, leaning over me as he presses me back, our positions reversed though I don't remember him flipping us. His hand grips my crotch tight, and rips. Coolness washes over me and he swears again. "Christ, princess. You're fucking flooded." Dark eyes latch onto mine as he presses his thick cock to my entrance, fluttering and swollen. We both groan when he pushes into me, hard and straining.

"You're so wide," I gasp out, locking my legs around his waist as far as they'll go. My legs are still encased in latex where he grips my thighs tight, burrowing deep in my slicked heat.

"So tiny. So fucking tight," Drake grates, pulling

back to slam all the way in. His thighs rest against mine and he groans. "Fuck, that's good. So hot, Cha Cha. Christ, you can own me any damn day."

"Mine?" I stroke his hair back from his brow, the single word a question that tastes light on my tongue. I consider it for a moment, then nod. "You're mine, now," I whisper, not needing volume to claim him.

Drake's eyes darken impossibly. He grips my hips in both hands, slamming into me.

I want to scream but can't, every cry choking on a breath that refuses to release. My nails dig into his shoulders, struggling to grip onto him in his frenzy.

"I'm yours, Cha Cha," he rasps out. "Not gonna let anyone else have you."

The promise in his words sinks bone deep as he pulls back and flips me onto my stomach, pushing my knees apart. Then he's buried inside me again, his weight settled over my body.

I cry out into my forearms, my pussy pulsing on his swelling cock. "I need—" Every word evades me, each breath too shallow for more.

"You're fucking mine, princess. I'll give you what you need. Everything. I promise." His hand closes gently on my throat, arching me backward.

I cry out as I come for him, clamping down on

his cock that impales me. Drake swears as I gush over him, his rhythm rough and brutal. His shout ricochets back at us as he fills me and then we sink together. Inked arms cradle me as he pulls a quilt from the bed to cover us.

"We're not moving for a while, princess." His soft words are the sweetest promise in my ear as he slides a hand to my hip, pulling me closer, his semi hard cock still inside me. "And when we do, I'm gonna fuck you until your voice rasps so that the next time you sing for me, I'll remember every scream I earn from you tonight."

I moan softly as he turns my head and kisses my mouth for the first time. Gentle at first, his lips press mine open, sliding his tongue inside. What starts so sweet devolves into something filthy and urgent. Drake kisses my mouth like he tongued my pussy through my latex pants. I moan against him, letting him take what he needs, stroking my tongue against his softly.

It seems to be what he needs. His cock hardens inside me, though this time, when he moves, he loves me slow and rough, exploring my body. I take every inch of him, and he shows me what sort of endurance my bodyguard really has.

CHAPTER ELEVEN

CHA CHA

My ruined latex pants lie in a puddle under my top in the bathroom. A trail of oil droplets and who knows what else follows my path to the shower. Steam fills the space as I shampoo my hair and lather my skin. The room is obscured by puffy clouds that block out everything—the walls, the mirror— leaving me in a dreamscape space where I can pretend I'm alone, just for a moment. I know Drake waits for me outside, keeping an eye on the door. He always does. There's security in that, but right now, I need to be clean.

Close to scalding water cascades over my skin. I need it, just to wash the oil from the latex off me, though I don't want to clean away Drake's touch. I ache in so many ways, all of them good. My body has never felt so used, so thrashed.

Despite the lovers I've taken from my previous bodyguards, I have never, not once, been with a man anything like Drake.

I've never been kissed by anyone like Drake. I've never been loved by anyone like Drake.

I've never fallen in love with a man like Drake.

I close my eyes, letting the water block out the world. I've fallen in love with the most unyielding, relentless man I've ever met. The man who stalked me. The man who, I suspect, might just love me back.

It's impossible and everything I want all at once. But I have no idea if what I want is the same thing that he's chasing. The man who draws away from everything, all the way out here in the mountains, and only comes out to play, taking security contracts and changing careers as it suits him.

"You're fucking mine, princess. I'll give you what you need. Everything. I promise."

The thought that he might, *just might*, want me like I do him leaves me hot all over again. Facing him on that front is a different matter. I want to hide away from him and never bring it up but... also I can't hide here forever. We have to go back. Even Shayne hasn't emailed me, which either means he's scared of me, Drake or a bit of both.

If he's scared of Drake, I don't blame him. I am too, sometimes, but in a good way.

He's still intimidating as all hell, though.

I let the spray wash the soapy lather away once I'm satisfied that I'm oil residue free, relieved that the hot water lasts long enough and I'm not left in an icy deluge scrubbing away instead. Reaching blindly for the taps through a fresh plume of steam, I miss the mark and hit a solid, hard surface instead. A quick feel around reveals abs and a chest. Not bare, but I can work with that.

A smile quirks the corners of my lips as I tilt my head back, hoping for one of those kisses that floored me before—literally.

"You can't join me if you're clothed." I pluck at his shirt. The damp material pulls away from his body and springs back with a wet slapping sound when I let go. "Though I'm a bit sore after two rounds so fast, Mister bodyguard."

"I don't remember you having nicknames for me." The deep voice so close to me is one I recognize.

But it's not Drake's.

"Major." My eyes fly open. "What are you—" I

back up a step, straight into the shower wall. *Mistake.*

Major Barret crowds the space with his bulk that looks twice as big as he did when he was my security detail. Heat that has nothing to do with the shower creeps up my body from my legs to my neck, my skin prickling.

You left. You can't be here. You aren't—

The letters.

But Drake said you were his friend. Visiting?

He's in your space. You're freaking naked.

There's a connection.

It's you.

Don't let it be him.

But it is.

My mind gets it, even as I'm still trying to find a logical reason for my ex-lover and bodyguard to be in Drake's house, standing here with me while I'm showering. Naked.

Unprotected.

My mouth opens, my shriek ready, but nothing expels from my throat over the hand that grips it.

My voice.

My breath.

Major smiles, his face partially obscured from the steam that blooms around us. Water pounds over his head as he shoves me backward. He closes his hand tighter around my neck, cinching every fragment of breathable space from my oesophagus.

"I thought it would be hard, entering Drake's space to take you. But maybe I don't need to take you after all. Because he's got you, so you're...not fucking mine anymore, are you, Cha Cha?"

I scrabble at his hands, trying to remember what Drake told me to do, but I'm not sure we ever covered being choked in a shower cubicle. Sure, he showed me how to throw a punch and how to knee someone in the balls—to his detriment several times—but never to free myself from someone nearly twice my height, with an arm's reach that means that even if I do kick him, I'm unlikely to strike anything useful.

I try anyway, and Major laughs. "Cute, sweetie. Almost as cute as the tantrums you used to throw. Remember those? All the times you ruined dressing rooms and I'd clean them up for you. All the times you used to sit and cry and I'd wait til you were done then pick you up and take you home. Fuck you when we got there. Leave you covered in filth because no one else was there to see." His voice bounces off the walls, echoing back at us. The fragments of our pasts haunt me.

"Drake," I cry, only it comes out as a splintered whisper at best. At worst, he'll never hear me. Us. Not over the running water.

Drake, where are you?

Probably cooking in the kitchen. I thought he was watching for me, but the man seemed intent on feeding me up. And here...he thinks he's untouchable. I thought so too. With Drake...

I'm safe.

Tears fill my eyes and tumble over, the salty drops washed into my mouth, diluted by the constant stream of water cascading over both of us.

Major's fingers flex on my throat. "Little slut, shacking up with every security guard you hire. What's that been now, Cha Cha. Four, five? How many will there be after Drake?"

"No one," I managed to croak.

Major glares at me. "Damn right there won't be anyone. No me, not another single man will touch this body. Fuck, for the year I put into guarding you, all you ever did was fucking mope around, sing and throw fucking tantrums and cry. You do that for Drake, too? He put up with you?"

Clarity slams me at the same time that major cuts my air off entirely. Two answers I can't give him that my ex bodyguard doesn't want, but I do.

First, that I haven't had a tantrum in the entire time that I've been with Drake. With him, I don't need to. Nothing about him leaves me bereft of emotion, unloved.

Second, I have my answer. Drake doesn't put up with me. We work quietly side by side, sharing space together. He's let me into his home, his life. He's shown me a part of him and shared stories that I doubt he's told anyone else for a long time, if ever. I treasure those moments, and now I know.

In the minute before I die.

"I love him."

My confession makes no sound. I have no idea if Major understands me or not. I don't care. The heat in the bathroom intensifies. I swing weakly at him, clawing his un-covered arm. Major snarls, arching over me. One twist of the hand clenched around my throat, and he'll snap my neck.

I force my eyes open, intent on focusing on the man before me until the moment I can't any more. The man I once thought I might love who turned out to be little more than a pretty facade, filled with trophy photos and brag comments shared to his friends across the industry.

"You are nothing next to Drake," I wheezed, smiling into Major's shocked face. Red suffuses his features, rage and hatred written in the lines of his face.

Once I thought you were beautiful.

Once I wished you were mine.

The hand on my neck draws me forward, then shifts me back. My head thunks the shower wall twice before he's done.

Who's having the tantrum now, Major?

My eyes close after that, and I let my body slide down the wall. He seems to be happy. My head splits with the sort of pain that heralds a migraine, and gravity is ten times heavier than it should be. My body shakes, and the water is cold.

"Drake finally ran out of hot water, huh?"

But I don't know if the words come out of my mouth, if I imagine them, or if the water is hot or cold anymore.

I don't know anything at all.

Certainly I don't understand when a heavy weight slams over me, knocking what little air is left in my lungs straight from my body.

I cough, and someone swears.

"Christ, princess. I'm sorry. That wasn't the way I meant for him to fall. Come on. Up with me." Broad arms I know intimately wrap around me, I rest my cheek on Drake's shoulder, letting him slide me out from beneath the world's heaviest weight. "Fuck, Cha Cha. You're covered in— Jesus. I'm sorry. I wasn't here in time. I was—" Drake swears again, easing me in his arms.

Bright light leaves my eyes watering. I wince. "Ow," I croak, and flinch at the hideous sound that comes out.

Drake's horrified face comes into view. "Come on, princess. I got you. Let's wash you off over here." He takes a cloth and pats at my face. I try to turn my head but my neck hurts. And my shoulders, and my back. "Don't try," he murmurs. "Everything's gonna be sore for a really long time. I'm sorry." Regret lines his face. "Fuck, little queen. I'm so sorry I wasn't there." He places a gun on the bench top and rinses out the cloth, nestling me against his shoulder.

I try to twist to look over at the shower, but he turns me away.

"Don't look," Drake says in a low voice. "He can't hurt you. Not anymore."

"He knew—"

"He did. He wrote them. The letters. I found one on your bed." A muscle works in his jaw as he washes my face and then, with the sort of tenderness I've never experienced in my adult life, Drake touches my throat. "I'm sorry, princess. Let's get you some ice."

I swallow as he wraps me in a dry towel and carries me from the bathroom. The pain consumes me for a full minute as I struggle between the action, choking on my own saliva, and breathing. "L–l–"

"I'll get you water." Drake wraps an icepack around me and pulls a blanket from a chair, wrapping me in that too. He refuses to put me down, and I nestle deeper into his chest.

"L–l–"

"Don't talk," he murmurs. "Save it, princess."

I glare at him, and inhale through my nose the best I can. "I fucking love you," I rasp out. Something aches, like I tore something in my throat, but I get the words to him.

Drake stills for a fraction of a second, then his mouth descends on mine in a sweet kiss that leaves me more than breathless. "Love you too," he whispers back. "But right now, I have to fuss over you and fix this mess that should never have happened in my home. Here, you should have been safe. I know," he strokes my cheek, and adjusts my ice pack — "I know that he knew us both. I know you were with him."

The conversation from our first day together sits between us. A shadow flickers across his eyes.

I hate that, and tap his chest. *"No,"* I mouth. *"I only love you."* I poke his chest with one finger to make my point, doing my best to conserve my voice but get it through his head at the same time.

Drake watches me carefully. "Same, princess. Are there any other ex-lovers I have to take out in this quest to be your one and only? Because I'll do it." He kisses the corner of my mouth with extreme care. "Promise."

That last word is said so softly I barely hear him even though it's only us here, but that makes it all the more solemn.

"I believe you." I make sure he's looking at me so he sees my mouth move.

Drake follows the words with his eyes, and smiles. "That's good, princess. You keep believing in me, and we're good." His smile fades after a moment and I know he's hurting too.

Hurt that someone got past him in his own place, when he thinks he should know better.

I frown, gripping his shirt and pull.

Drake doesn't budge. His eyebrows rise. "Got a problem, Cha Cha?"

I wrinkle my noise, lever my way up and press my mouth to his.

The sound he makes is feral, brutal and everything that I love about him and that scares me at the same time. *Everything.* I sink back into his embrace as he makes a blanket puff of us both on the floor.

And that's how they find us: his security friends and my management team, a few hours later. My icepack has melted, but Drake's arms never let me go.

And in that time he's told me everything I need to know about him. Where he grew up, all the missions he was never supposed to talk about. His seafood allergy, the pets he had as a child. What toppings he hates on a pizza. His front door is broken down by a guy he calls Hendrick, who actually kicks it off its hinges. He has a woman in tow, a tiny birdlike musician who talks to me for the next hour while the mountain house is invaded by more people than I've seen in weeks.

Before they arrive, my bodyguard even whispers his last name to me, giving me the secret I've craved for so long.

It's Drake.

EPILOGUE

DRAKE

Cha Cha dances about the stage like it's her personal boudoir shoot—only in front of a hundred thousand fans all screaming her name. It took a year for her voice to return to normal under strict coaching and exercises, and in that time, I coached her too. She's now proficient in self-defense, several martial arts styles and carries a mean punch as well as knife throwing. That last ended up as a feature in her latest music video that landed her an award that she thanked me for both publicly and in private.

The latter part was fun.

I don't break into her stage work, unless necessary, and that's rare. I watch her from the wings, a small set of screens showing me the arena from her point of view, as well as who is nearest the stage. But I keep a personal eye on my girl, and she often looks across at where I stand, knowing I never take my eyes off her.

"Fifty seconds," the new stage manager says in my ear.

Her last crew all moved along—voluntarily—along with her sasaeng, though one of those ended up with silver bracelets when I tracked through each personality profile and cross referenced those with activity logs from the stadium of the night I took her away with me.

I wasn't convinced that Major Barret was the only active stalker hunting Cha Cha the night he broke into my house. That she knew him and that he knew me bothered me for days after we figured the connection out. Afterwards, the twisted romance and the letters started to add up. I understood how easily someone so close to her could become obsessed.

Hell, I was halfway there myself. But our love developed in other ways. Major, after they broke up, bragged about the celebrity he fucked and left to his friends. That *use and abuse her* mentality devolved into something else entirely. He could claim he walked away with no feelings hurt just like Cha Cha, but at the end of the day, he wanted her back, and so down the rabbit hole, his emotions dived.

Cha Cha is worth every twisted heart, every obsession, after all. But while she might be the celebrity clause in several relationships, she's also the sort of obsession that, globally, leaves hearts broken and tears on cheeks whenever she releases a new song.

Like tonight's.

Sometimes, her obsessed fans go a little too far.

But the shattered mirror and the message written there that I pieced back together before she turned up in her dressing room that first night never suited Major's M.O. not when I looked back on his profile.

But that profile did suit the sasaeng. And when I interviewed them, one at a time, I found some discrepancies that matched up with the blacked out portion of the security footage for her dressing room that night. The pink and white haired pastel fanboy was carted away without either fanfare or objection. Actually, he appeared kind of thrilled with his adventure, which sickened me somewhat.

After that, Cha Cha's team underwent voluntary cleanse. The only remaining staff member is Shayne who is now Master of the Wardrobe—his official title—a choice by both himself and Cha Cha. That seems both pompous and overdone to me but they love it and who am I to complain? My girl is happy, and so am I.

"Twenty seconds." The voice in my ear is far too chipper.

I nod, concentrating as Cha Cha sings through the final chords of her new song that she closes her most recent tour with every night.

> Once I thought you were beautiful.
> Once I wished you were mine.
> Now I know you're broken inside,
> Nothing but show and shine.

The lights black out on the stage. I step back as the team we handpicked and interviewed together flood the area. Everyone has a designated spot and I'm anal as hell about people staying in their lane.

Cha Cha waves to the crowd and belts out her planned encore after making the audience beg for it. I smile at that; she's growing stronger in asking for what she wants. The rest of the close off runs as planned. I follow her back to the dressing room, opening the door and checking first, then stepping aside for her to enter. No sasaeng or wannabes sit in the quiet, empty waiting room. It's just me and her new manager who hangs about, tablet in hand with tonight's remaining schedule.

Which had better involve a shower and sleep.

Cha Cha doesn't so much as glance at me as she enters, already talking to Shayne about what worked for her costuming and what didn't. We keep everything public and professional about our relationship. A handful of people know, and so far, we've managed to keep it out of the media, mostly so Cha Cha isn't barraged with questions she doesn't want to answer yet. If that shitstorm blows up, then it does, and we'll face the media together too.

Her fingers brush my thigh in the lightest touch. That's all I get in acknowledgement, but it's enough. I pull the door shut behind her, Cha Cha talking animatedly as she unzips the side of her costume, tossing her hair over her shoulder.

I swallow hard, forcing myself to remember that this is her space, and that we'll have time together later tonight if she has the energy, or tomorrow, when she's not performing or on the road. Maybe I can cook for her, seeing as she barely eats when she's on tour and stressing about every detail.

I'm halfway through a menu for tomorrow when the door opens beside me and Shayne steps out, followed by a stuffed capybara that sails over his head.

My eyebrows hike. "Tantrum?"

It's been a while since I saw one of those in action. Cha Cha had a few when her voice didn't work the way she wanted early on. It was a toss up on whether she'd go for the plush toys or throwing knives, but that was back home where we could duke it out together in a safe environment.

He runs his hands over his curly pink tinged hair. "She wants spangles for the next tour. Fucking spangles! We're not in honkey tonk land." He bares his teeth, looking like a deranged ram.

I shrug. "So, let her have them."

He glares at me. "This is your fault. You indulge her."

That's probably true. I shrug. "She works hard." It's the cover we put in place early in. Shayne has always suspected, but never called us on it outright.

"Yeah? Then you can deal with her *hard work*. It's you she wants, anyway." He pouts like a spoiled child.

I snort. "She doesn't always get what she wants with me," I mutter.

"Okay. Fine. You convince her to put the damn latex into the next act she performs, then. She's all yours." Shayne storms away, taking Lola, the new stage manager, with him, cussing not so softly under his breath.

Crouching down, I collect the upside down capybara, and turn for Cha Cha's door. *Latex, huh?* The memory of the night I showed her what a good-night kiss could be like leaves my blood hot in an instant.

I knock on her door. "Cha Cha?" The handle gives, and I push it open.

A stuffed tiger zooms past me. I duck by reflex as a plush potted daisy follows it. The next airborne item is a fluffy pink pig. I catch that and kick the door shut, flicking the lock.

"No mor—" Something white and gray slaps my pec. A squeaky shark bounces off my chest. I don't bend to pick that up. "Ow, princess."

Cha Cha turns to me, her wide eyes framed with thick black lashes from her stage make up. "I. Wanted. You." She stamps her foot in her long white boots that encase her legs to her thighs in leather.

I know, because I zipped the fucking things up earlier.

"And I'm here."

"You are." She holds a stuffie in front of her as though she's unsure if she's about to throw it or cuddle the damn thing.

I take a step closer, tossing the two plush toys I'm holding behind me. "Tonight was too much?"

She shakes her head.

"You hated the idea of latex?" I try again.

She glares at me. "I don't give a fuck about the latex."

I stop and stretch my hands out at my sides. "Alright, princess. I'm outta ideas. But if you throw that at me at point blank range, it's probably gonna sting—"

The stuffie bounces off my chest and falls to the floor between us.

Cha Cha looks at me expectantly.

I sigh. "Come here."

She steps forward, sliding her feet beneath the offending toy in a carpet of the damn things. "I missed you."

My knuckle slides beneath her chin, but I let her tip her head back herself, unwilling to hurt her accidentally. I know she's recovered but I can't not see the necklace of bruises left on her flesh because I didn't see the threat when I should have.

"What do you need from me tonight, princess?"

I ask, reaching across with one hand to flick off the light, but keeping contact with her so she knows where I am.

The room lunges into darkness, and suddenly, she's gone.

"Cha Cha?"

Warmth blooms across the front of my suit pants. I groan as she mouths my cock though the material, her tongue teasing the shape of me. "Fuck, princess. You could have said."

Her giggle undoes me. I sink my hands into her hair as she works my belt free, then the zip on my pants. When my cock touches her lips, I tip my head back, digging my toes into the soles of my shoes.

"Christ, princess. Keep teasing me and I'll paint your face with my seed. Then everyone will know," I murmur.

Her soft sigh before she envelops my cock with her hot, wet mouth is the sweetest kind of torture. I massage her scalp, forcing myself to treat her gentle as she sucks me, putting her pretty little mouth to the best use. Within moments I'm aching, and wishing I hadn't turned out the lights. Her mouth opens wider and the tip of my cock hits the back of her throat.

She chokes softly and I pull her back. This isn't

something we've practiced, but she shakes herself free of my hands, and swallows me whole again.

"Jesus," I whisper, stroking her hair back from her face. "Little queen, I won't be able to hold back if you keep swallowing me like that. Are you sure—"

Cha Cha buries her nose in the front of my pants, and chokes.

My balls tighten, tingles racing along my spine. I swear not seeing her is worse, or maybe better. The image of her choking on me embeds in my mind. I grip her shoulders, pulling her up to me roughly.

"Too much, princess," I grate, lifting her in my arms. She's tiny, so easy to toss around. Her legs fit perfectly over my hips as I back her up until she hits the wall. I notch against her heat, and push all the way, slow, in one thrust.

Cha Cha buries her face into my shoulder, her scream lost in my shirt.

"Don't you ruin that voice, or you'll be explaining to Shayne," I withdraw to slam back into her again, "why you have red stripes across your pretty ass from my belt. Do you want to talk that through with him, princess?" I give up trying to fuck her nicely and rail her, praying the wall is sturdy.

Cha Cha meets me, relaxing her body so she slides along my cock without resistance, letting me delve deeper into her slicked pussy each time. The cries lodged in her throat are muffled, but her hold on me tells its own story.

Pleasure rips through me as her little pussy milks my cock. I growl my need against her mouth, kissing her gently even as I fuck her fast and hard. She kisses me back and then we lose all sense of control, tongues tangling as she gushes hot and liquid on my cock.

It's too much, the extra slicked sensation. I slam deep, searing my name on her walls. Cha Cha whimpers in my arms, panting and the sort of mess that will be damn hard to explain walking out of here later.

"Tell me there's a shower," I murmur, once my breath settles. "Or you'll be explaining a new factor in your show life to the media come tomorrow, princess."

"I don't care."

Those three words come from the tangle of arms and legs and sweat between me and the wall.

"What?"

Cha Cha tightens around me, leaving me groaning. "I. Don't. Care." She locks her legs around my waist, wiggling closer. "I don't care if they see us together. I don't care if they know, Drake. It's us. I'm sick of hiding."

My blood heats fresh. "You're ready to tell them?"

And by *them*, I mean the whole fucking world. Because there isn't a soul out there who doesn't know who Cha Cha Min is, or that's how it seems most days. If she announces this, or someone photographs us holding hands getting in the car tonight, or—fuck my life—us kissing, it'll be every-where before the morning editions hit the shelves.

"Yes, Drake. I mean I'm ready. I've been ready for a while." Cha Cha's hips wriggle.

Hell, this girl knows me so well. I'm already hard with the thought of her telling the world about us. Not having to hide who we are together any more. I did it because that's what she wanted and I got it. I supported her in every way. But being able to be us wherever we are? That's what I want. Sure, it comes with threats of its own but that's nothing we don't face on a daily basis. This simply changes the face of that landscape.

I catch her chin in a firm grip. "Cha Cha. Tell me you're sure."

She leans forward and presses a kiss to my lips,

already rocking on my cock. "I'm sure, Drake. It's why I—"

"The tantrum." I grin and tweak her nose, pinning her hips to the wall and burying myself deep until she moans, holding her there. "Better?"

"So much," she whimpers as I move slowly, eking every inch of pleasure from her that I can.

"Show me how much, princess."

Her body undulates with mine. I catch her mouth in a kiss that matches our movements, driving deep. Her slick coats us both as we find an edge and stay there, drawing out the pleasure before we tip over it together.

And because I'm a selfish bastard with a celebrity crush, I steal her sounds for myself, kissing her until my own need tears through me. Her name is on my lips as I seat myself inside her, staring into the eyes of the woman I love, with a side serve of obsession that she doesn't seem to mind.

THANK YOU
FOR READING

Thank you for reading Cha Cha and Drake's story! Please leave a REVIEW.

If you love possessive protectors and high spice, Z BOYS is fast paced, filled with snark, and sassy tension from the first page. Start with KING.

ABOUT THE AUTHOR

USA Today Bestselling author Sofia Aves writes fast-paced police romances, sizzling military units, steamy cowboys with a Montana backdrop and the occasional cheeky god. Sofia writes kidlit for charity and has over one hundred and fifty publications across six not-so-super-secret pen names. As acquisitions editor for Evernight and Evernight Teen publishing she loves discovering new talent in romance and YA spaces, and is a mum of three crazies in a returned veteran household. Sofia has two overly large fur babies who think they're teacup puppies, a duck who prefers to eat from a dog bowl and two axolotls named after a dragon and a firebird.

Sofia lives near Brisbane, Australia, where she has her own alpaca park, Lorendel.

www.sofiaaves.com

Sign up to <u>Sofia's newsletter</u> and get a free Blue Blooded Brothers book.

Haven't read the Z Boy's prequel? Get it for free here:
A TABLE FOR TEN
Follow Sofia on
BookBub
Twitter
Instagram
<u>Facebook</u>

READ SOFIA'S SERIES

Blue Blooded Brothers

Collision

Politics & Paperwork

Blindsided

Sentinel

Mugshots & Candy Canes

Impact

Reckoning

Red Hart Ranch

Snow on the Range

Siren on the Range

Sundown on the Range

Spirit on the Range

Ash on the Range

Mistletoe on the Range

Forgotten Mountain Man

Texan Devils

Ranger's Wish

Ranger Bedevilled

Ranger's Passion

Ranger's Fury

Ranger's Wrath

Ranger's Storm

Snapdragons & Seductions

Summer with a Ranger

Merry with a Ranger

Beach Duty Collection

Playing to Win

Off Boarding

Vicious Slash

Zero Pointer

Off Stage Fling

Rippton Allstars

Crushing It

Glacial Force

Rippton Creatives

Study Games

Make Me, Break Me

Twisted Obsession

Spring Break with a Mafia Prince

A Royally Fake French Menage

Angel Shot
Jericho Chimeras
Puck Me Always
Puck My Heart
Puck me Sideways
Z Boys
King
Joker
Hearts
Ace
Mayhem & Mistletoe
Ruski
Fast Track to Love
Speed Trap
Klauss Brothers
Zander
Keegan
Gallo Empire *with Jade Marshall*
Splintered Vows
Fractured Vows
Fierce Vows
Savage Covenant

Rom Coms
She's A Hot Christmas Mess
Boats, Moats and Root Beer Floats

Writing Romantasy as

SOFIA SHELLEY

Dead Poets Sorority

Writing Reverse Harem Dark Romance as

DOVE PRIEST

Recurve Ridge

Kidlit writing as

JO SEYSENER

The OCD Elf

The OCD Elf's Great Reindeer Calamity

Greg and the Egg

writing YA as

JOSS PHOENIX

Alchem Academy

HIDE FROM US

Writing spicy paranormal romance as

RAVEN HUSH

Club Fray

Darkest Desires

Purge

Kidnapped By Claws

Ruin

Shadow Lords

Sinner's End

Heaven's Gate (2026)

Monster Brides

Phoenix's Eternal Flame

Kraken's Vow

Krampus' Christmas Bride

Silent Sentinels Duet

Reflections of Silence

Echoes in the Void

Monsters In New York

Feral Moon Rising